THE LAST ENGLISH PLANTATION

THE LAST ENGLISH PLANTATION

JAN LO SHINEBOURNE

PEEPAL TREE

First published in Great Britain in 1988
This new edition published 2002
Peepal Tree Press Ltd
17 King's Avenue
Leeds LS6 1QS
England

ISBN 1 900715 33 3

I was wondering if I could find myself
all that I am in all I could be.
If all the population of stars
would be less than the things I could utter
And the challenge of space in my soul
be filled by the shape I become.

Martin Carter

1 THE INVITATION

Boysie Ramkarran tapped the gatelatch. Lucille Lehall, six months pregnant, looked up from her washing. Her daughter, June, was playing on the new six-foot water tank in the far corner of the yard where a bushy guinep tree grew and sheltered the tank, only recently tarred, from the sharp mid-morning sun.

'Good morning,' Boysie's deep voice cut through the peace and quiet. He called out to June, 'How Muluk?'

June saw her mother straighten and drag her soapy arms from the wooden tub. She saw too her look of coldness and dislike as she went to the gate and spoke to Boysie. 'Yes?'

'I was wondering if Cyrus might be home,' Boysie said.

'Cyrus is always at work at this time of day.' Lucille spoke her English English, rounding the vowels so that her accent changed completely and distanced her from Boysie. 'And please don't call June 'Muluk'. That is not her name. Her name is June.'

'Muluk' was the name Nani Dharamdai Misir called June by. Up to this year she had been called both names in New Dam, but her mother was putting a stop to it now that she was going to go to school in New Amsterdam. Some people said 'muluk' meant 'India', some said it only meant 'place'; whatever, Lucille did not like it.

Knowing he was not wanted, Boysie turned and walked away, back to New Dam village. He was a big man with strong shoulders and large arms, who marched rather than walked. Had he been pale, Boysie would have passed for an overseer like Overseer Sam Cameron. Both men wore a thick moustache curled at the ends, both wore khaki clothes, both looked bullish and fearless, but their difference was in their race and position. Boysie lived in the village, was a Hindu and a boiler at the factory, Cameron was a Scotsman, an overseer and he lived in the European quarters.

Boysie always put her mother in her worst mood. Now she was scrubbing so hard on the washboard, her knuckles were bound to be tender afterwards. For the rest of the day, Boysie's effect on Lucille would linger. She would continue to speak English English and demand of June that she speak like this too. She would snap at her frequently: 'Speak proper English!' meaning not correct grammar and vocabulary, which she had taught June well – Lucille's father had been a Lutheran pastor, a convert from Hinduism – but the imitation of an English accent, which June lacked. It embarrassed June that no one else in New Dam spoke like Lucille.

That afternoon, the English Overseer, James Beardsley called on Cyrus Lehall. On his afternoon walks with his Alsatian dog, Overseer Beardsley did not always confine himself to the European quarters, sometimes leaving the asphalted road to cross the High Bridge into New Dam. When June heard the overseer calling from the roadside, she fetched her father from the kitchen where he was making a cup of tea, then she leaned from the window and listened to their exchanges. Cyrus remained on his landing while the overseer remained at the roadside. For a while the two men exchanged small talk, then turned to what the men on the estate always talked about: work.

'The three-eights draglines have arrived from Georgetown,' the overseer informed Cyrus.

'Oh yes?'

'It will mechanise irrigation completely.'

'They already have dragline up by Veira plantation on the East Coast, by I does meet up with the mechanic fellow that side I hear 'bout it.'

'Oh yes, Cyrus, they're making quite an impact...'

'Will put some fellows out of work bad.' The overseer listened while her father named all the men and boys in the shovel gang, who would be made redundant by the draglines.

8

'And that is why the mechanising 'in altogether a good thing,' her father was saying. 'You see, although I is a mechanic, I could appreciate how it puttin' my mati out'a work. Look, in my father day everything was manual. Was pure cutlass use to clean land. Shovel use to dig drain, was oxen long ago use to plough before tractor come. People use to do all forking and half-bank-and-plant, creole gang used to do all fertilising, we had weeding gang, people doing all reaping, bundling, punt-loading. People had was to even walk to canepiece befo' lorry come. Now tractor got disc and harrow to plough, fork, till an' everything. Now crawler tractor diggin' drain, now is chop-and-plant, not half-bank and plant, now airplane will start sprayin' fertiliser soon I hear, not shoulder-tank, an' tractor will start pullin' punt soon. I hear even bulk-loading coming to factory and factory self going to get bigger to help increase production capacity.' He laughed nervously. 'Well yes, factory getting bigger, more sugar getting produce but you need less men to do it because of all the mechanising. What a t'ing. Grinding season going get longer, and ratooning too. From 25,000 capacity, I hear we going aim for 50,000 capacity. I hear everything going change in factory too, from juice, clarifying, evaporating, crystallising...'

Although her father said he did not like Overseer Beardsley calling on him, when he did, he could not stop talking. More plantation talk followed until June found herself not listening any more, then drifting inside to light the lamps and the mosquito coils.

That night, Boysie returned with some of his men. The family were at their dinner when they heard Boysie call up. 'Come Cyrus, come man. We want to talk to you.'

Lucille gave her husband the look of reproach she really wanted to direct at Boysie. 'Tell him you still having your dinner.' She never used her English accent with Cyrus.

Cyrus left his half-eaten dish of hassa and tomato curry and went to the window. 'What it is you want, Boysie?'

Boysie's voice reached them again. 'A talk with you, Cyrus. Come down, man.'

'I eatin' dinner. You have to wait.'

Cyrus returned to the table and resumed his meal, but Lucille was now in a bad temper, her meal spoilt by Boysie's presence outside. Sitting near her, June sensed all her tension.

Lucille declared, 'That man has no manners, none at all.'

Cyrus sighed and drank from his cup of water. 'Maybe they come to arrange for the weeding on Sunday.'

Cyrus was always hopeful that Boysie and his men would join in the work of maintaining the village. Since the Sugar Industry Labour Welfare Fund had been established, the local government paid the village councils a small amount to maintain the villages. The Fund also provided other advantages but New Dam was slow to take them up because Boysie and his men were hostile to it. They felt that the fund as well as the Village Council had been created by the Governor and the overseers. Boysie argued that it let the estates ignore their financial responsibility to maintain the villages; they should spend the sugar profits on paying the workers a good wage instead of pocket money on a Sunday.

Lucille knew all this. She told Cyrus, 'I doubt Boysie will help with the weeding.'

After dinner, Cyrus descended the stairs to meet Boysie and his men. June went to the landing and looked on. At this time of night, seven o'clock, it was the kerosene lamps in the cottages which provided all the light. There were only four lantern posts along the public road in New Dam, one here outside their house which was Lot no.1, the others strung out at equal distances to the end of the village. Theirs was the first house which you came to when you approached New Dam, going towards New Forest. By nine o'clock the village would be covered in darkness – fuel was expensive. Now, with all the lamps alight, the cottages, yards, paths and greenery were fretted with light. There was noise too: dogs barking, crickets and frogs calling, the humming of William Easen's small electricity generator next door. Sometimes you could hear Mr. Easen's large Ferguson radio, the only radio in the village, when it was working. A baby was crying, children were still playing in the yards and the noises of cooking and washing could still be heard. Any visits to be made, anything to be discussed, had to be done now, between seven and nine, between the last meal and sleep.

Cyrus asked Boysie, 'What I can do for you, Boysie?'

'I hear that Overseer Beardsley been here to see you this afternoon.'

There were five men with Boysie, not all from New Dam, only Jagbir and Tulsi were from New Dam. This year, Jagbir was working as a casual labourer – June had overheard her father telling her mother this. Jagbir worked half at the sugar estate, half at the rice mill, the sort of thing that made a worker unpopular with the overseers. They could ask him to leave the plantation and live somewhere else. Jagbir could be without a job and a home next year; this was why he followed Boysie, who liked to take up the cause of such men.

Cyrus asked, 'What that is to you?'

Boysie replied, 'It is important we know what these over-seers want when they take it on themselves to walk into our villages.'

Cyrus challenged him, 'What do you think Beardsley was doing? You think he was asking me to burn down New Dam or something?'

Boysie laughed, 'You naive you know, Cyrus. You don' work on plantation so you don' appreciate...'

Cyrus's voice rose with impatience, 'Look he' man, don' talk to me as if I is some fool, man. I know what is what. My father work on this estate all his life.'

'As a foreman...'

'He start off as a stableboy and work hard too fo' people rights.'

Judgements about the rights and wrongs of their families, family honour, always entered the conversations between Cyrus and Boysie. Both men were born in New Dam. Cyrus's father, Lou, was one of the few Chinese men who had stayed on the sugar plantations as labourers. Lou had worked his way up to a foremanship, earning himself a right to live in the junior staff compound where the standard of living was much higher than New Dam's, though much lower than the Senior

Staff compound where the overseers lived. Lou had chosen to stay in New Dam with his wife, Jaswanti, who had been an orphan from the Essequibo, whom he had married by arranged marriage. Up to the age of eighteen, Cyrus had worked on the estate as a mechanic's apprentice. Now he was a self-employed mechanic, sharing a workshop at Palmyra Village with two others.

If Cyrus had not been so involved in community affairs – the maintenance of the dams, petitioning for electricity and water supplies as well as medical and educational improvements – Boysie would not have had so much cause for confronting him, for they had been schoolfriends. There was one important difference between them though. Cyrus knew and understood Hindu customs, but he chose not to practice them, and his marriage to a Christian finally separated him from Hindu practices. Boysie, though not a devout Hindu, did maintain some customs. Often, he could be seen in his yard in the morning doing his puja, sprinkling water at the rays of the sun. Cyrus had been taught these customs by his mother. In his childhood he had spoken Hindi, his head had been shaved twelve days after his birth, and the Pandit had consulted the *patra* and chosen a name for him, Dushyand, after one of the kings in the Shakuntala stories. Up to her death, his mother had called him by his Indian name, and by hers, Narain, which meant celestial light. Boysie had called Cyrus by his Indian name when they were children but now used his Christian name.

Cyrus asked Boysie, 'When you going help we weed the parapets and clean the drain? Whatever happen we still have to fight unsanitary condition and disease. If we don' build up the backdam, all them house aback goin' get flooded and old Jairam and Charu sickly an' can barely move in they house.'

'Tha's na' we job,' Boysie retorted. 'Is the blasted estate fault the bleady canal floodin'.'

'I don' disagree, is their job, but they not doin' it, and the Welfare Fund giving money to do these jobs on a Sunday, we may as well do it. Sometimes you have to act in emergency and fight another time, Boysie.'

Boysie insisted, 'Now is the right time to fight. They introducin' cut-and-load, doing away with cut-and-drop. Now them boys going get they back break rass. You know how them canebatch heavy? Now they gat to hoist them 'pon they back an' carry them sometimes so much hundred yards to punt! Overseer don't want pay people to carry the cane no more so cane-cutter got to carry it now! You 'in see overseer t'ink we no better than brute animal?'

'I support you against cut-and-load one hundred percent.'

'You tell Overseer Beardsley so when he been here to visit you today?'

'Yes, I tell him so.'

Boysie sucked his teeth in disbelief. 'And what he say?'

'He say he think it bad too.'

Boysie laughed loudly. 'Good, I glad to hear it. Let he tell Manager Smith them too and let all'a dem take they backside outa this country.'

'They will go. One day, our own government will be running estate. I not worried like you whether the overseer will go or stay. I know this going be the last English plantation...'

Boysie muttered darkly. 'Last one in truth...' There was a pause. Boysie had found out what he wanted but he would leave only after he had had the last word. He turned and pointed in the direction of the forest. 'They used to have plenty Dutch plantation up the river. African slave rebellion and river finish them off one by one. This is the last plantation lef here in Canefields.' Boysie slapped his chest. 'I am the man will make sure this is the last English plantation.' With that, he turned and walked back to the public road with Jagbir, Tulsi and the others. But something was nagging him. He turned back and called to Cyrus who had moved away from his gate:

'You sure he didn't come here to spy? You sure din' say anything 'bout guns? Overseer McKenzie tell we how they storing up guns to stop we striking. Them British soldiers and warship bring plenty guns – McKenzie tell we so.'

Cyrus laughed. 'Guns, Boysie. Well you really believe this is cinema. McKenzie like to threaten people. He want you to

13

believe he. No man, Overseer Beardsley come yesterday on personal business.'

Boysie returned to the gate. 'Personal? What *personal?*'

Cyrus said, 'He got a sick daughter June age. He ask if June could go an' visit she, see if she could raise the child spirit.'

Boysie sucked his teeth. 'Wha' you want send you child to overseer house for? Let he find overseer child to play with overseer child. You is Chinese and Indian mix and you wife is pure Indian. How Beardsley could ask you? He should ask he own mati...' Boysie now turned and left finally.

On his way into the cottage Cyrus ruffled June's hair. He went to the kitchen where Lucille was scrubbing the pots. He put a pot of water on the kerosene stove and lit the fire, then he sat at the table to wait for it to boil. June sat opposite him but he avoided her eyes.

She had never visited the European quarters. Until now, her whole life had been spent in the village, at school or at home. Occasionally she accompanied her mother on a shopping trip to New Amsterdam. Every New Year's eve a busload of villagers usually visited New Amsterdam where they could walk up and down the streets gazing at the bright christmas trees which were displayed in the windows of the houses there. The young men would join in bursting balloons and firing squibs in the street. In a month she would be starting secondary school in New Amsterdam. Her feelings about it swung from excitement to anxiety.

The flame under the pot was licking round the sides, blackening it. It would be another pot for Lucille to scrub. Her work never seemed to end.

Cyrus spoke to June. 'Young lady, it's time for you to go to bed.'

She contradicted him. 'I don' want go.'

He commented, 'You too own-way.'

She asserted, 'I not going to no Overseer Beardsley house.'

He gave her a cutting look. 'Who told you anything about you going to Overseer Beardsley house? You been listening to my conversation? And anyway you will do as you are told, whatever it is.'

14

She shouted, 'No!'

Lucille stopped scrubbing and came to the table, her apron damp, her soapy hands clutching the handbrush. 'What's this?'

Cyrus sighed. 'When Overseer Beardsley visit he ask if June could go and visit his daughter, the sick one, Annie.'

Lucille frowned deeply, 'He asked you?'

'Yes.'

'That is strange. Why he ask you?'

'I don't know.'

June said, 'I don' want go no overseer yard.'

Her mother shook the brush at her. 'Speak properly. Say 'I don't want to go', not 'I don' wan' go'. I've told you, I won't listen to anything you say if you speak it so badly. You're starting school in New Amsterdam soon and if you go there speaking so badly you will be left back in your work. You know very well how to speak proper English. Why you prefer to talk that terrible Creole?' She sighed, turned and returned to the kitchen sink.

language

The sink was a large wooden window box which she had to lean over. Two enamel buckets of water always stood at the ready, along with the bars of Zex soap, Vim and wire scrubbers which she used. Lucille busied herself again with scrubbing the day's used pots. Her household labours and her ambitions and hopes for June and the child which she carried inside her fretted her enough without Overseer Beardsley adding his family worries to hers.

It was difficult for June to be angry with her mother. Her anger was mixed with love, especially now as she watched her with her bulky womb covered by the dirty, wet apron, pressed against the window sill, her face worn and tired from the day's work. Although there was bread in the bread bin, tomorrow she would rise at four in the morning to cook a hot breakfast of roti, dhal and calaloo and shrimps for Cyrus – a meal he would also take to work in a saucepan for his lunch. The early rising and cooking was a custom of the poor Indians, the one custom of his mother's which Cyrus liked Lucille to retain. Now Lucille was calling, 'June, come and help me wipe and put away these pots.'

Her father insisted, 'No, let her go to bed. Is late. I will do it.' He pointed June in the direction of her bed, then went to his wife, took her arm and drew her away from the sink. 'You should leave these pots till tomorrow or just scrub the outside twice a week. You don' have to have the whole pot shining like silver every night.' He sucked his teeth wearily, took up the towel and began to dry the pots. 'You should be resting more now, not less.'

Lucille's mind returned to Overseer Beardsley now. She said, 'I don't understand why he should ask us. The senior staff is full of white children and the local overseers' children, and there are girls in the junior staff compound June's age.'

'He said is because Annie going start school at New Amsterdam High School too, like June. A lot of those children are Roman Catholics and will be going to the Catholic schools, and other children will be going to the non-religious school. That's what he said. But he said too that Annie don't have friends. I think he said she used to go to the Catholic school in New Amsterdam but had some trouble there. He said too his wife is a strong Anglican. I suppose because you is an Anglican and June goes to church too...'

The mention of June and church only irritated Lucille. She declared, 'June is a heathen. Mistress Beardsley is wrong to think she is a good Anglican. You should tell Overseer Beardsley the trouble I have getting her to go to church. The devil has that child soul. She prefer to go to the Hindu weddings, matikore, to kali-mai and queh-queh, but come Sunday morning you know very well she locks herself in the latrine or the bathroom. You don't set her any example. You only ever went to church when we got married and when June was christened. As for your language, you don't bother to speak English...'

He sighed. 'Lucille, you just letting off a lot of steam. Let us come back to the matter at hand. Beardsley say Annie gets bullied, can't stand up for herself. What we going to tell him?'

Lucille snapped, 'So we, June, is just her last chance?'

Cyrus sighed. 'The girl sounds very sick. Beardsley say she don' eat at all. He is a worried man. I feel very sorry fo' him.'

'Let him send her to a doctor in England.' Then she

recanted. 'It sounds bad, really bad. What could make a child like that? They have a big house, all the facilities. Mistress Beardsley have servants, she can take care of her children. What is she doing about it?'

'He said she try and try but can't get through to the child at all.'

'It sounds very strange to me.'

June said again, 'I don't want to go,' pressing her parents to refuse the Beardsleys.

Cyrus seemed not to hear her. 'To tell you in truth, I feel sorry fo' them.'

June repeated, 'I not going.'

Both her parents gave her a look of rebuke and her mother said, 'When there is sickness and you are asked for help you must never refuse. It is one thing you never turn your back on. Families must help each other.'

June disagreed. 'The overseers not our family.'

'No, but they are still *families*. Being overseers don't mean they not human. Not all of them are bad, and certainly Overseer Beardsley is the best we ever had. I don' know how he ever turn overseer.' When she became introspective Lucille lost her uncertainty. Now she was lapsing into her natural voice and was not conscious of it.

The pot was boiling. Cyrus prepared two cups of green tea and a cup of cocoa for June. Lucille came to the table and sat down next to June, then opened the large tin in the centre of the table and drew out the two elongated loaves of bread. Cyrus brought a jar of guava jelly and a tub of margarine to the table. From the shelf June took down plates and knives. Lucille prepared the bread. This was the last ritual before they retired to bed.

Cyrus said, 'Boysie tell me we must not send June there.'

Lucille frowned. 'What did he say?'

'That they are white and we are not.'

'That man is so racial,' Lucille commented bitterly.

'Boysie is not really racial. I t'ink he was really talking politics. You know how people always mix up the two. He was only reminding me Beardsley is an overseer.'

17

'Say what you have to say without making excuse for Boysie. I don't like him. He has no right to be passing comment on what we should or shouldn't do. I detest that man. He has no interest, either, in improving our living conditions. He just likes to bear grudges, to fight. You know what his name means? The last part of it – karran – means fighter, but the first part, Ram, means he is a man in the service of god, a fighter in the service of god. Well, Boysie like to fight for the sake of it which is why some people call him by the name Karran and not Ramkarran. He makes me ashamed to be his race...'

Cyrus cautioned her, 'Don't talk with so much passion, Lucille. You allow Boysie to upset you too much. You think he is critical of you but I never heard him criticise you. Is just his way of life you don't like, especially the way he keeps women in their place.'

'He thinks he is lord and master...'

'We not talking 'bout Boysie really. We talking 'bout Beardsley and the thing he ask us.'

The smell of the mosquito coil was now strong in the cottage. The village was darkening as the lights began to go out. June felt her eyelids heavy with sleep. There was only one bedroom in the cottage. She slept in the corner of the partition which separated her parents' bedroom from the rest of the cottage.

Cyrus drew in his breath and turned to June. 'I think you have to go and see how you could help out, June.' Then he yawned deeply.

2 THE VISIT

On the day that June was to visit Annie Beardsley, her mother washed, starched and ironed her best dress and, at five o'clock, she set off on her cycle for the quarters where the overseers and their families lived.

That part of the plantation was divided into senior and junior staff compounds large enough to hold four of the workers' villages. The Manager, Bill Smith, had the largest house, which stood on fenced land large enough to take one village. He lived there with his wife and several servants. Their children were at school in England. Overseer Beardsley was the second deputy manager. His house, his land and trees were half the size of the manager's. The first deputy manager was a Scotsman, Edward McKenzie, whose house, land and trees were in exactly the same proportions as Overseer Beardsley's. The other overseers lived in small family and bachelor bunga- lows which were maintained by workers and patrolled by security guards. All these overseers and the managers were called 'senior staff'. Formerly they had been only English, Scottish, or Welsh, but it was now the practice to employ and house in the European quarters one family and one bachelor of each Guyanese race.

The junior staff were local people, workers who were at a level between the overseers and the labourers. They worked in the office, the dispensary and in semi-professional positions. The junior staff compound was crowded with cottages only a little larger than the cottages in the villages, but they were furnished by the estate, and enjoyed running water, electricity, and maintenance services provided by the estate. Like the local overseers in the senior staff compound, the junior staff were a new class of people.

All this was separated from New Dam village by the sideline canals and shrubby wasteland where a few coconut trees grew. In the middle of this space stood the Anglican church and the cemetery. Canals and drains separated the living quarters. Often, the overseers could be seen on their verandahs surveying the flat land around their compound with binoculars. The overseers' quarters were guarded strictly. No one could enter without a security check. In the grinding season, the canals and culverts were patrolled by security guards.

Ten minutes of cycling and she reached Overseer Beardsley's house. There was a security guard at the gate. He telephoned the house, then opened the gate and waved her in.

She rolled her bicycle in and began to walk. The guard encouraged her: 'Cycle up, cycle up, is a long way in.'

The bicycle was unstable on the gravel path. She passed a poui tree, then a row of flowering shrubs on either side. The further into the garden she moved, the more it enveloped her. It was very cool because there was so much shade from the sun. The light breeze spread the perfume of the flowers everywhere. None of the plants or trees looked in need of care; they bore no dying leaves or branches. The borders were clean and raked, the huge green lawn a carpet which spread itself into the corners of the garden. All the flowers which her mother loved, and some which she had never seen, grew here: powder puff, poinciana, cassia, both pink and yellow, pink and yellow poui too, poinsettia, lilac, jungle geranium, jasmine, bougainvillia, and there were roses, orchids, lilies, ferns and unfamiliar plants with coloured leaves.

Lucille loved flowers as if they were her soul; if she had been granted the time and space to cultivate them, it would have been as if her own soul flowered. Their yard in New Dam was cluttered with as many fruit trees and vegetables as they could fit in: mango, guinep, starapple, papaya, gooseberry, guava, golden apple, pepper, calaloo, corn, bhaigan, same, ochroes, squash, peas, shallot. Lucille could only squeeze in the flowers and decorative plants in pots and hanging baskets, nailing them to the trunks and branches of the trees and along the front and back stairs. Grass was an enemy in their garden; it took up too much space. Here in the Beardsley's garden there were several standpipes near the fences, and long green hoses trailed from them. Lucille had to pay the small boys in New Dam two cents for every bucket of water they fetched from the standpipe to keep the garden watered. The fetching of water from the pipe was one of the jobs June had done as soon as she could carry a saucepanful of water. Now that Cyrus had built the new water tank it would be easier.

June rolled her bicycle under the bottomhouse and noticed then the small cottage which stood beside the house. This was the head servant's cottage. It was painted white, with white lacy curtains in the window and a green zinc roof. The small garden round it was decorated with whitewashed rocks and flowering plants. The door of the cottage opened and a servant appeared, in a green dress, white apron and hat. She looked at June, said nothing at all to her and walked up the back stairs of the house.

After a few minutes another servant, dressed in the same uniform, appeared on the stairs. She signalled June to follow her and led the way upstairs. The door was covered in green netting in which were entrapped a few dead flies and mosquitoes. When it was closed behind her June found herself in a kitchen four times the size of her cottage.

'Hello, you must be June.' The English voice belonged to the woman who was leaning against the sink. She was preparing green plantains for making chips. June guessed she was the wife of Overseer Beardsley. She spoke again, this time to the younger servant. 'Claudette, give June a glass of lemonade.' Then she pointed to the chair which stood between the refrigerator and the door, 'Sit down, you must be tired from cycling.'

The chair was very hard, the back straight. When she sat in it she found herself wedged tightly between the door and the refrigerator. There was the warmth of the sun on her right arm and the cold of the refrigerator on her left. Claudette brought her a glass of cold lemonade. Mistress Beardsley returned to peeling and chipping the plantains. The two servants were working quietly. Claudette was wiping the dishes again and the older woman was sweeping the floor. There was silence between the three women as they worked.

Mrs. Beardsley peeled and cut the plantains expertly, like a local woman. She was tall and thin with short, wavy, reddish-brown hair. Her eyes were very blue, her nose crooked and thin, her lips thin and red, her face thin, her skin slack and lined. She was not beautiful but her make-up and dress made up for it. Women in the village did not wear make-up like this. Her face-powder, rouge and lipstick were subtle and June knew that Lucille would admire the cut as well as the quality of her dress. Lucille used only face powder, the same she had used since she was a young girl. The women labourers wore no make-up at all except for blackpot, the soot which women collected on the cooking pot which they used as eye shadow. The young women who experimented with cheap make-up brought by salesmen from New Amsterdam were labelled 'wild' and they did use the make-up wildly, rubbing rouge thickly on their cheeks and eyelids and so much lipstick their lips became red slashes in their faces.

Mistress Beardsley spoke to her again. 'So you will be starting secondary school soon?'

June nodded.

Now Mistress Beardsley took off her apron and wiped her hands. 'I will fetch Annie now.' She turned to the older servant, 'Mavis, put the oil on now please and cook the chips when it's the right temperature. Use fresh oil please.'

'Yes ma'am.' Mavis answered.

June waited with the refrigerator humming in her ears. The servants pretended to ignore her. Soon Mrs. Beardsley returned to the kitchen.

'Come, June.'

A long, wide corridor separated the kitchen from the rooms at the front of the house. June was led into the middle doorway, into a room larger than the kitchen. Through the row of open windows she saw the view through which she had just cycled. The public road was almost hidden from view.

This room was as much a dream as the garden and the kitchen. The chandelier, the three large mirrors on the walls, the glasses in the cabinets, the ornaments, polished floor – all were clean and shining in the light which poured through the windows. The wooden walls were painted cream, there were no bright colours here. There were large armchairs and a settee with brown cushions. The paintings on the wall were of sea-views which looked English, windswept and cold.

Mistress Beardsley turned to the doorway and said. 'Here's Annie.'

Annie entered the room but remained leaning near the doorway. Her appearance gave June a fright; she was unnaturally white.

Her mother took her hand. 'Don't lean, Annie, stand straight. Come and meet June who's come to play with you. June is starting at the same school as you are in three weeks.' Now she spoke to June. 'You and Annie play downstairs. June you go first, then she will follow.'

The front door was nearest. June made for it but Mistress Beardsley stopped her. 'No, use the kitchen door.'

June walked through the kitchen and caught the servants laughing. She ran down the stairs.

In the garden she sat on the bench under a poinciana tree. The house was full of what her mother called 'facilities' – the piped water, electricity, the refrigerator, the stove, washing machine and other machines larger than June thought they would be, larger than those she saw in the shop windows in New Amsterdam, and china, cutlery and furniture in quantities. June decided she did not like it here at all. It was strict and unfriendly because of Overseer Beardsley's wife who liked to give orders, and all the space seemed wasted.

Annie came slowly down the stairs. She was as thin as her mother. Her hair was very white. She resembled her mother with the same thin face, nose, lips and eyes, but there was life in Mistress Beardsley's face, look and movements, plenty of life, there was none at all in Annie's. June could only compare her to very old, sick people, but Annie was a child. She stopped at the bottom of the stairs. June did not move. She felt as if

23

Annie were a bird or some rare creature she did not want to frighten. She pretended to ignore Annie and slowly the white girl began to walk towards her.

Annie sat on the grass, a few yards from June, in the shade of a cherry tree.

She spoke to Annie, 'Ants on the grass.' Annie did not move and she repeated herself, 'You have ants on that grass. If you don't move it will bite you.' She wondered if the ants were biting Annie and she could not feel them. 'You hear me? Ants, ants and bete-ruche.'

A sound of giggling behind her made June turn around to see another white child leaning and laughing against the dwarf coconut tree. This had to be the other Beardsley child, the one who was not sick. Her eyes were as blue as her sister's and hair as white but her eyes were lively and her hair was full of untidy curls. Her skin was red from the sun. She wore a pink and white dress that was fussy with ribbons, puffed sleeves and smocking. 'Bete-ruche?' The child was shouting and laughing.

The child was laughing at her and she could not tell why. She swung around and pretended to ignore her. The child ran towards her and sat on the grass, a few feet from her sister.

It's not bete-ruche, it's bête-rouge. It's French and it means red beast. And we don't have ants and bête-rouge on our grass because our gardener puts something in the grass to kill them.'

June's shame melted away. So that was why the child was laughing, because she used the wrong word. She did not care. People in New Dam said 'bete-ruche' and as long as they thought it was all right, it was all right. 'I don' care!' she snapped.

'What's your name?' The child demanded.

'Is none of your business!'

'I know anyway! June Lehall!'

'So why you ask me if you know! Stu'pidy!'

'You don't speak properly. You pronounce all your words wrong.'

'I don' pronounce no word wrong.'

'Oh yes, just listen to you.'

The child was going to find one reason or another to criticise her. She was trying to get the advantage over her. June was not going to let her do it. She went to the coconut tree and picked several leaves off a branch.

The child warned, 'I will tell the gardener!'

June ignored her and took the leaves over to Annie. She sat beside her and began to strip the leaves off the woody stem which was used to make brooms in New Dam. With the leaves, June made the elaborate Amerindian whistle which all the children in New Dam knew how to make. As she worked she described the technique to Annie who stared at her fingers. When she finished she blew the whistle. It made a soft, flute-like noise. She adjusted the pointer to increase the sound and when it pleased her she placed it in Annie's lap and looked towards the west, gauging the position of the sun to see if it was nearly six o'clock – the time when her mother said she must leave for home.

June asked Annie, 'You want to play?'

Her sister shouted, 'She can't play! She's not well. Play with me.'

June said, 'I will play catch.'

'What's catch?'

June found five small bricks and showed her.

The child laughed. 'That's Jacks. In England you use a rubber ball and five metal pieces.'

Irritated, June snapped. 'Well this not England and we use bricks.'

One of the servants was making her way to the cottage. It was the older servant, Mavis. She called out: 'Sarah, I hope you behaving yourself.'

'Yes!' the child called back, in a rude voice.

'You better had!' Mavis warned, then she began to sing.

They played 'Catch'. June won seven points out of ten.

Sarah did not like losing. She pouted and her lower lip quivered. Then she noticed the bicycle.

'Give me a ride on your bike!' She demanded.

'You don't have any manners?' June asked.

'Please.'

'Anyway, no. Is a brand new cycle. My parents buy it fo' me to ride to school; I not allowed to lend it out.' June looked at the new watch on her wrist – also a present for passing her exam. It was quarter to six, fifteen minutes more before she could leave. 'What's your age?' she asked Sarah.

'You should say, 'How old are you.' Not "What's your age?" That's incorrect.'

June sucked her teeth in exasperation and Sarah sucked hers back even louder, but she turned and looked in the direction of the cottage.

'You frighten Mavis!' June taunted.

Sarah sucked her teeth again, knowing June had found her weak spot.

'How old you are?' June demanded.

'Ten!'

'You big for your age.'

'Not big. I'm not big, I'm tall!'

June got up and went to the Madam Yass tree. She plucked several of the bare green branches and took them back to Annie. Again she sat near her and showed her how to make a necklace. She placed the necklace in Annie's lap. Still, Annie did not seem to notice.

Sarah complained, 'You really should not pick those branches. We are not supposed to do that. That tree is very precious to Mummy, that Parkinsonia.'

'It name Madam Yass,' June contradicted.

Sarah's eyes widened with surprise, then she began to giggle derisively again and exclaim, 'Madam Yass!' over and over again.

'You really stupid,' June commented.

'That tree is named after the English botanist who discovered it, Parkinson. It is not called Madam Yass.'

June decided to leave now. She got up and began to walk to her bicycle.

Sarah ran after her. 'You can't go yet, not without telling Mummy.' Then she ran upstairs, shouting 'Mummy, she's leaving without saying goodbye.'

She waited with her bicycle until Mistress Beardsley and Sarah descended the stairs. They were holding hands; Annie was still sitting on the grass, the whistle and necklace in her lap.

26

'Thank you for coming, June,' Mistress Beardsley said, then she tugged Sarah's curls. 'I hope Sarah wasn't misbehaving. She is very wild. Sarah, walk with June to the gate.'

As they began to walk along the long, winding path, June saw Mistress Beardsley go to Annie, take the toys from her lap and help her to her feet.

'What wrong with Annie?' June asked Sarah.

June noticed how it took Sarah a few seconds to work out what she was saying. Words did not mean the same thing to them. It only showed how cut off the overseers were from New Dam, from all of Canefields and, from what Overseer Beardsley told her father, from New Amsterdam too.

'She sick?' June repeated.

'She's ill.'

'Ill with what?'

'Leukaemia.'

'How you know?'

'Mummy said.'

'Your mother told you that?'

'Yes, and she may have to go to England.'

'Then why she's starting school? People with leukaemia don't go to school.'

'Don't ask me that. I don't know.'

'I don' think you know at all. Leukaemia does kill people.'

Sarah changed the subject. 'Which primary school did you go to?'

'St. Peter's.'

'Where is it? In New Amsterdam?'

'No. Good Land.'

Sarah laughed mockingly and said, 'Mummy says the poor coolie children go there and they have millions of lice in their hair and that you have to use latrines there. And that you all get beaten with whips. And you all smell of coconut oil, and you use cow-dung, you daub it on the earth where you live.'

Anger burned in June. She stopped and looked at the child, feeling sick and distant from her. She pointed her finger at her. 'You! You are a bad, wicked, evil little child! God will punish you! You will roast in hell for your nasty nasty mind! You should count your blessings and feel humble for what you have instead of slandering poor people who can't help themselves. You should feel shame! You wicked, nasty, wicked, shameless child! And who tell you to call people *coolie?* Who give you the right to call people *coolie?* They are *not coolies* They are workers and if they did not work you would not have what you have!'

Sarah's face became stricken with horror and she began to weep. June did not enjoy the sight of the child's terror and horror. She took her arm and shook her to stop her weeping.

'Look, take the bicycle, take a ride! Stop crying, man!'

The offer of the bicycle dried Sarah's tears. She wiped her eyes on her arm and clambered on to the bicycle. June held the bicycle steady, then walked it towards the gate.

Sarah talked freely, 'Annie used to go to the convent school in New Amsterdam. All the children on the estate go to the convent school – they are all Catholics. They are all local Portuguese children. The English children like us would prefer an Anglican school but we have to go there, but we always go to England afterwards to school there. But Daddy wants us to stay and go to school here. But Annie hates it. They bullied her at school and she doesn't like the estate children so that is why they sent for you, so she would have a new friend at New Amsterdam High School. I don't go to school. Mummy teaches me at home. She gets books from England. She and Daddy quarrel a lot about where we should live.'

'How you know your parents quarrel?'

'I hear them at night in their bedroom and at lunchtime on the verandah when they think I'm sleeping. Annie hears them too.'

June rebuked her, 'You should help to look after your sister instead of trying to take away her company from her.'

Sarah looked hurt and June saw that there were two opposite sides to her, a side which was cruel and a side which was soft. There was no in-between to her. She either laughed at people or was hurt by them.

They were not far from the gate when Sarah pointed to the bushes at the far corner of the fence and asked her to guide the cycle there. When they reached the bushes, Sarah jumped off the bicycle and disappeared into their midst. June could hear her giggles. She stood the bicycle on its stand and as she approached saw that a small hole had been cut into the bushes to form a hiding place. A blanket was spread on the ground and there were dolls which she had seen in the shop windows in New Amsterdam: a teddy bear, a golliwog, a blonde doll and a clown. Sarah opened a large wooden box and drew out books, a mirror, hairbrushes, handkerchiefs and a pair of binoculars. 'This is my spying quarters,' Sarah explained. 'Everyone has binoculars here. They are always spying on each other when it is the workers they should be spying on, Mummy says. So I spy, I spy on the coolies and niggers...'

'You want your mouth scrubbing out with coal tar soap...'

'Mummy says I am articulate,' Sarah declared stubbornly.

June did not know the word 'articulate' but she knew another word which it sounded like, 'artificial', which Sarah was. 'You talk too much.' she commented. 'And most of it is nonsense. You can talk all right but you should learn to talk sense. No point having plenty words and no good sense to make with it. Plenty people in New Dam can't talk like you but only talk sense.'

Sarah's lower lip quivered. June had hurt her and she was going to cry again. June fled from the hiding place, took her bicycle and began to ride towards the gate. Sarah recovered quickly, ran from the bushes and began to chase her. The security guard left his hut and came to the gate. The girls reached the gate together.

Sarah shouted at the guard, 'Don't let her out! You are not to let her out!'

He threw his head back and laughed loudly, opened the gate and shut it after June, commenting, 'That child mad, both'a dem mad.'

3 OLD DAM

Outside the gates, June turned and studied Sarah Beardsley who was pushing so hard against the high wire fence it sagged under her weight. Now the look on Sarah's face was like her sister's – a dead look, a look that made June feel as if she herself had put them there, behind the fence. Being anxious to be on her own way home made June feel this all the more sharply. She hopped on her bicycle and crossed the public road, turning towards New Dam. Behind the wire fence Sarah Beardsley began to walk in the same direction. When June rode faster, Sarah ran, keeping her eyes on June all the time. She ran as far as the end of her garden, where a narrow drain divided it from Overseer McKenzie's land. At the high bridge June turned around one last time to see Sarah pressed against the wire fence, still looking for her in the distance.

Apart from the factory chimneys and uppermost storeys of the overseers' houses, this bridge gave the best view of the surrounding landscape. She had been born here, in the logie village which used to occupy the land on the south bank of the canal, with the factory on the north bank. Her mother had told her that when she was born it was the grinding season and the noise from the factory had drowned her cries. The village used to be called Old Dam. Now the ground was abandoned and flattened. Nothing had been put in its place and when she stopped here to gaze at the desolate landscape her memories of Old Dam revived and peopled it again. But her memories were disturbed today by Sarah Beardsley and the scornful things she had said about them.

She leaned her bicycle against the wall of the bridge and sat in a corner of the wall, with her legs dangling over the water.

The sweet smelling breeze, perfumed with cane, washed her face. It was true that they used latrines and not flush toilets like the overseers and junior staff and people in New Amsterdam, but the DDT men came with shoulder-tanks every week and sprayed all the latrines and drains. It was true that the children at primary school had lice in their hair and she had caught lice often. It was true that the children used a lot of coconut oil in their hair and on their skin. It was true that they used cow dung mixed with mud to daub the ground in the bottomhouses. Coconut oil was preferred because the coconut was a sign of good fortune which families included in their goodwill wedding offerings. The cow, and everything it provided, was sacred too, including the dung. The overseers used grass lawns to cover the earth round their houses but the villagers used a cowdung and mud mixture to keep the ground from cracking, to keep it smooth and soft to walk on. Lucille did not use coconut oil or cowdung. She bought sweet-smelling soaps and perfume and was forever scrubbing and attacking everything with bleach and disinfectant.

Why was she feeling sorry for the white girls? There was a traitor somewhere inside her to make her feel sorry for them. All this August and September, a boredom that was new and strange claimed her days. All her old school friends were in their villages, working in their homes, at the saw mill, on farms in the Corentyne and some were even working in the fields and factory although they were legally too young. One day they were there playing and doing their best at primary school, the next it was over and while she was waiting to go to school in New Amsterdam, they were gone to work. In the mornings, lying in her bed, she rehearsed the school register – Indian names on one side of the register, Christian names on the other. She used to enjoy hearing the teacher read the names because they had a music and rhythm she liked which the English words of their lessons did not have: Fiazullah Aziz, Pratima Asregadoo, Vijay Beharry, Sawati Bhattacharria, Drupati Budhwar – then she lost the alphabetical order: Mariam Armogam, Somar Kanhai, Chandra Mongroo,

Rajendranauth Bissoondyal. Then came the Christian names: Joyce Patterson, Henry Archibald, Alexander Charles, Cordelia Rodney, Patrick Liverpool, Aloysius Goodenough. When her mother overheard her rehearsals of the register and lessons she would tell her that talking to yourself was the first sign of madness. Lonely for the rest of the day she would buy chalk from Mr. Romotar's shop in Adelphi and use the watertank as a blackboard, pretending to be one of the teachers, usually Mrs. Lawrence who used to be her favourite teacher, and address her invisible schoolmates who she imagined were seated on the ground around the watertank. She was lonely now like the two white girls.

Now that she was going to go to school in New Amsterdam like the children of the overseers, her mother said that if she took her education and did well she could be anything she wanted. She could be a doctor, or a lawyer, or a teacher – anything at all. Although Lucille was careful not to say it, June knew she meant that she could leave New Dam where it was not possible to be anything but poor, which meant being scorned and treated, as Boysie said, like an animal. Boysie said that the overseers made them live like animals, as if they were not human. His solution was to make the overseers leave Canefields, not the workers, the people who had lived there all their lives.

Some people said that things had improved and were still improving on the estates. But Boysie said that things were getting worse. She did not know who to believe. In Old Dam they had lived on a mudflat without drains and walked barefoot in the sticky mud when it rained. The cottages were jammed close together and people could lean from one window or door into another. The logies were choked with large families. Lucille hated to remember it. Yet June's memories of it were happy. She could remember that she was never alone, even when she was home from school. Her life there was surrounded by children and it made her happy to remember how they had played from morning to night, a complete world of children. She spoke Hindi in those days, until Lucille and St. Peter's school erased it from her tongue. It was because of the Hindi that Lucille had spoken perfect English to her constantly, until it hypnotised her. It was the reason for the books too. Lucille got Ali to bring second-hand books from New Amsterdam in his bus: Grimm's fairy tales, out-of-date encyclopaedias and dictionaries, dress catalogues from England and America, English farming manuals, newspapers and magazines, cookery books and old Georgetown newspapers. Ali had done this favour three times. Each time he kept the stack of literature on the shelves in the bus, forgot them for weeks while they became dirty and torn from being trapped between baskets of goods, then when they did arrive they had to be cleaned and salvaged. Lucille liked best the assortment of religious books with hypnotic illustrations of angels, heaven, hell, paradise, Jesus, God and the saints and characters of the bible. June turned over the pages of these books and learnt to know the textures of each page, each cover and their different prints. She read entranced, lured into the fantasy of new worlds, always feeling afterwards as if she had eaten too much and needed to run and play outside. Schoolwork had the same effect. It all erased the Hindi, the language of the coolies, the poor. The new language, English, did not only translate the books into her mind, it also translated New Dam. The more she absorbed the books, the more she became conscious that their words were not the words the people around her used about the same life, and she would listen for the differences. But then she began to understand that it was not just different words but different points of view she was really hearing. They each had their own point of view. Her mother's one ambition was to raise their standard of living even if it meant that June had to go to school in New Amsterdam. Her father expressed all his feelings and ideas through his work and talk about work. His Sundays were spent with the work-gangs weeding and cleaning and repairing the parapets, drains and dams. William Easen, next door, wanted to make New Dam Village Council work independently like the village councils on the West Coast and the Corentyne. He spent all his time trying to convince people how important this was. Nurse Nathaniel was interested in the health of Canefields. Nani

Dharamdai taught the Hindu religious outlook to everyone; she gave religious pictures to Nurse and Mr. Easen for their Christian christmas. But when Nani began to teach her how to perform morning puja, Lucille stopped her visits there and sent her now only on necessary errands, like the exchanging of fruits, vegetables, groceries and advice on cures and treatments for illnesses. There was a complicated situation between Nani and her mother. Nani treated Lucille like an adopted daughter in part because her parents were dead, but more because she had lost her Hinduness. Sometimes Lucille resented it, sometimes she did not, but now that June was going to start school in New Amsterdam, Lucille was even more against it, and June had never heard her express so much prejudice against Nani and everything she stood for as she did these days.

She did not think she had her own fixed point of view yet, she was still young. In your youth you were supposed to get experience first, but Sarah Beardsley had a fixed point of view about them. If Overseer Beardsley was such a good man and liked the poor so much, why did he allow his daughter to scorn them? Why was she the opposite, why did she like Old Dam so much? Yet when Sarah scorned her she felt ashamed, the shame of being poor and having to live with latrines, lice and coconut oil. She did not want that shame. How did she come to have it?

She stopped her thoughts, raising her eyes from the water and letting them follow the line of the horizon from north to south. There was so much space in what she saw and yet their lives were so fretful. The landscape before her was a solid wall of sky and land. You could walk and walk and the land would never end and the sky would stretch further and further away from you – that was how walking on the backdam felt; the land was bigger than you and the smell of water followed you everywhere: creek, river and canal water. It was as if it was too big to hold people and they worked it until it turned into their grave.

She began to remember the day Old Dam was turned into the flat empty place it was now. On that day the bulldozers had come and flattened the logies and trees. None of the overseers had come to see Old Dam bulldozed. They had sent men from New Amsterdam to do it. In the weeks before, Lucille had talked about the 'move' to come, explained that they were going to live in a nice cottage in New Dam where there were drains, four standpipes instead of one, yard space, and guttering on the cottages. They had packed their belongings and stood on the public road and waited until four red bulldozers came dragging themselves like crabs over the High Bridge. At first, June had thought they were on their way to the backdam but instead of turning left, eastwards, they had turned right and trundled towards Old Dam. When they reached the village, one of the women hollered at the drivers to wait, then she ran back to one of the logies. The whole displaced village had been standing at the roadside – the women, children and old people with their livestock: chickens, guinea fowls, and ducks in crates and coops. The pets: monkeys, parrots, dogs and cats, were moving too. The donkey carts and barrows on the road were loaded with their possessions. Half the people were going to live in villages beyond the plantation. They were the ones who had ceased to work for the overseers, who were not being found new homes and had nowhere else to go.

The woman had come running back, clutching a pepper tree in its rusty tin. When she was safely back among the watching crowd, the bulldozers moved in. When the first bulldozer was within a few yards of the first logie it had put out its huge metal sweeper like a hand, then the driver reversed, stopped, revved the engine and drove the machine with surprising speed into the front of the building which folded and collapsed into a heap of broken wood. He drove round and attacked the logie from a different direction. He did this several times until it was all a pile of shredded planks on the ground. The other bulldozers did the same to the other logies and cottages. Soon, a cloud of thick dust covered the scene.

While they were still bulldozing the village, the red lorries which were used for transporting workers to the Corentyne plantations and far-flung canefields arrived. They came over the bridge in a convoy of ten. They were empty except for the tenth lorry which brought a team of workers, men and boys. The trucks lined up near the ruins of Old Dam. The workers jumped off the lorry and began to fling the remains of the logies and cottages into the lorries.

They stood and watched like people at a funeral. June had tried to feel glad, like her mother, that they were pulling down the logies. She told herself it was not a clean place, that it was too near the factory which was noisy and dirty, smoke always pluming from the chimneys in the grinding season. Sometimes, looking upwards, seeing the great crane reach down and seize clumps of cane from the punts, she used to feel that an accident – a crane dislodging from its hoist and flying across the canal – could destroy their cottage. A fire in the factory could easily have spread across the canal, threading a path across the punts of dry cane, and consumed the village. The canal had become polluted too, though the children still swam there. Her mother was glad to see the last of the canal. But when June had looked up at Lucille to see if she was glad that Old Dam was being destroyed, she had looked stiff and serious in the straw hat which she used whenever she felt that she needed protection from the sun.

When the bulldozers had finished their work, they lined up along the canal and one of the drivers stripped to his shorts, stood on his bulldozer and dived straight into the water. While the drivers bathed, the workers loaded the remains of the logies into the trucks, then sat on the loads and ate their lunch from their saucepans. A little later, one bulldozer drove through the ravaged site towards a small grove of coconut trees. The driver lowered the metal sweeper to the ground then drove it into a coconut tree which snapped and keeled into the earth. The driver leapt off the bulldozer and began to dig into the wound of the tree for the 'heart' – a rare delicacy, which he sat down to eat contentedly. After the bulldozers and lorries had gone, some people returned to the site to grieve their loss. The others wished each other well and went their way.

Long after they moved to New Dam, June used to tell herself she was glad that Old Dam had been destroyed because to care then was to bear too much sorrow. She had not really counted her losses. Now, she remembered the life in Old Dam. Half the families in Old Dam had been African, living in cottages set a little way from the logies where the Indian families lived. Yet they had lived like one large family in spite of their differences, the women sharing childminding and attending each other's birth, marriage and funeral rituals. They all, men and women, used to gossip and talk work and politics. She missed the feeling of belonging to that kind of village. Now they lived in separate African and Indian villages. Things like the masquerade bands, part of the African life of Old Dam, did not visit New Dam.

She remembered the Harvey family. They were a family of teachers who had given an eagerness for education to many Old Dam families. Lucille had been close to them. When Old Dam was bulldozed, the Harveys had moved to Georgetown and Lucille had been left without their advice and had to make her own judgments and decisions about June's education.

The sun was sinking now, the landscape was shaded and cooling from the heat of the day. She rose, brushed the dust from her skirt and legs and continued her journey home. Lucille would want to hear all about her visit to the Beardsleys.

At home, she found her parents arguing in the yard. William Easen was with them, with one of his disused, portable generators. Lucille was grumbling at Cyrus. '...Well don't bother then. I don't care.'

Cyrus said, 'I just can't please you.'

They were arguing about the new lavatory again. Cyrus had bought all the parts from Davson's Stores in New Amsterdam. He had built the wooden closet for it in the bottomhouse and dug the ground, laid the pipes, and made the underground concrete cesspit, then Lucille had decided, after studying the foreign catalogues again, that she wanted the lavatory upstairs. The bottomhouse was not the right place for a lavatory, it was too public – anyone from the road could walk into the yard and use it. Cyrus said there was nothing wrong in letting neighbours use the lavatory. Lucille said the whole idea was to have some privacy. Then Cyrus had said that he did not have the skill to put in an extension upstairs or run the pipes there; they could not afford more materials. They argued over money and other technical problems.

Mr. Easen, who liked to be involved in progress, demanded, 'You all want this generator or not?'

'No point, Wills,' Cyrus said. 'The generator no good...'

'How you mean it no good? It only need a good service. The other one working.'

'That one always breaking down. Anyway, I can't afford no electric pump. Lucille crazy. You know how much a pump cost? Then we would have to pay engineer to put it in. I putting the lavatory down here.'

'Well help me hais' it back,' Mr. Easen said.

Together, the two men lifted the generator on to the barrow and steered it away.

Lucille looked frustrated. She always had to be working on something improving – it drove her. Now she turned to June and said, 'Go upstairs and change your clothes. Your uniform material come. I want to measure you and begin sewing it.'

4 THE UNIFORM

The material was the best wool and cotton they could buy, but June found fault with it. She complained that it would be hot and itchy, she would roast in it, she would look like a policeman in blue and white. When Lucille did the first fitting June would not stand still and a pin pierced Lucille's thumb.

'Fidget!' Lucille scolded her.

June complained how thick the woollen skirt was, how uncomfortable it would make cycling, that she had almost four miles to ride in the morning, then in the afternoon again, and another eight miles if she came home for lunch.

'What's the matter with you?' Lucille asked bitterly.

'I don' like this uniform.'

'Don't! Not 'don'! Speak properly!' She mimicked her mockingly: '"I don' like this uniform." Girls have been wearing this uniform for years, the best school in the whole county. If it were not a suitable uniform they would not still be wearing it, but it's not good enough for you, madam, oh no!'

'We wear a lot'a things that not suitable. Look at Mr. Shepherd always in his wool suit and sweating. Wool is for England where it cold.'

'Don' talk about England if you can't speak their language! Oh ho you is smart woman!' In her anger Lucille dropped her English. 'Now you making me talk just like you!'

The war over the uniform continued for a week. June escaped from the cottage to ride her bicycle around the village as often as she could, but if she stopped to speak with one of her old school friends, she frequently found herself in the way of their chores. And besides, Lucille was against her keeping up her primary school friends and her friends were now in awe of her. Her new bicycle, bought for her journeys to New Amsterdam, was a sign of her new status. She cycled to the saw mill in Good Land and watched the men and boys at work. The boys recognised her and waved, their faces and bodies covered with the fine dust of wood shavings.

This saw mill and the rice mill were the only two private industries in Canefields but they were run on a scale too small to compete or compare with those of New Amsterdam, the Corentyne or Essequibo. Mr. Easen said that a good village council would change that. Canefields was backward, he complained, living too much in the past. Cyrus always disagreed with him and argued that this part of the country was economically backward because it had never been drained and irrigated properly, and that gave the estate more control over people's work. If they had a village council, Mr. Easen argued back, they would get some of the help Cheddi Jagan was talking about giving to poor people in the country: the duty-free fertilizers and machinery and land on cheap leases – but Mr. Easen was also afraid that it would be the people who already owned land and were prospering who would take advantage of these opportunities, not the people they were intended for. If Jagan did not look out, he would create rich and powerful people he could not control and end up not helping the estate workers settle the land they had worked on like slaves for years. He called Cheddi Jagan a dreamer and Cyrus told him that he, Mr. Easen, was a dreamer too, to believe that the village councils could ever have so much power. Cyrus agreed with what Boysie said: the Development Plan was not a proper plan, no long-lasting improvements would come from it, people would only fight over the hand-outs and forget real politics.

At the second fitting of June's uniform, Nurse Nathaniel came to help Lucille. She watched as Lucille knelt beside June with a cluster of pins between her lips. There were bags under Lucille's eyes and she moved with difficulty, her womb now resting heavily on her thighs. When a pin pricked June, she shrieked resentfully.

'I don't know what is the matter with you,' her mother complained. 'You hardly feel that! You ungrateful child!' When June sulked, she continued to rebuke her. 'Don't swell up your mouth like some crapaud when I speak to you.' June swayed from side to side knowing it would provoke Lucille. 'Why are you doing that?' she snapped. 'Haven't I told you not to rock like that when you're spoken to; you will make the pin stick you again!' Lucille stopped the fitting and glared at June. 'Why don't you say you're sorry, eh? Say you're sorry!'

In the tense silence June's eyes filled with tears. If she opened her mouth to speak she would sob. Yet she had been wrong, not Lucille who was pregnant, exhausted and doing her best to sew her new uniform, to turn her out smartly for her first day at school. She felt bad and ungrateful and un-happy, and the mixed-up feelings stormed in her and brought the well of tears which made her heart beat, her chest tighten and her whole body go tense. She rocked herself to try to loosen her tension and beat back the tears. It only irritated Lucille more but she held her tongue and turned to Nurse for help.

'Nurse, what am I to do?'

Nurse looked uncertain and distressed, her eyes moving from mother to daughter, afraid to take sides. She and Nani Dharamdai were always called in to help settle family crises in Canefields. Although Nurse was an Anglican and Nani a Hindu they both visited homes of both religions, but Lucille had not sent for Nani, she had sent for Nurse. The Lehalls had never had cause to consult these women for family advice, only health advice, and because Nani lived here in New Dam and Nurse lived in Pheasant, Nani was the obvious choice. Nani understood the family better because she had known Cyrus's and Lucille's parents. Nowadays, although they hardly saw Nani, Lucille talked about her as if she was a threat, as if she was always interfering in their lives, which was not true.

Nurse was looking at June, eye to eye, as if she could read her thoughts exactly. June was not afraid to look back at her. Her face was handsome, large and honest and she sat back looking straight and relaxed, her arms open, her hands resting

41

on the couch. She made June feel that she could do anything, but she also made her feel exactly the child she was.

'Well are we prepared for this important, exciting new venture?' she asked June, as if she had only just entered the cottage, was greeting her for the first time, and had not witnessed the conflict just now.

'Yes, Nurse,' June responded, as Lucille had taught her to reply.

Lucille was relieved to hand over to Nurse. She went to the sewing machine and began to sew. This upset June. Lucille only brought Nurse here so she could wash her hands of her. There was no need to bring Nurse here. Nurse and Nani only went to people's homes when men beat their wives, daughters ran away with lovers, brothers and fathers molested the girls in their homes and people stole from each other and fought over livestock and various possessions. She had not stolen anything, she had not been violent or told lies like the Rambarran boy at Lot No. 12 or the Jonas boy in Good Land whose mothers had taken them to Kali-mai to try and exorcise the devil in them.

'You did very well to pass your entrance exam, June, very well,' Nurse said.

Nurse was saying it, but Lucille never said it. She just moved from one thing to the next. Once the fuss over the exam was over, a new one began over the uniform, how she should speak and should not speak, and whose company she should keep. She felt sorry for Lucille because she worked so hard, because she was still feeling sick after six months of pregnancy, and she even felt proud of her courage, but she was unfair sometimes, though June could not name this unfairness. Now she avoided Nurse's eyes.

'June, look at me,' Nurse said. 'Are you helping your mother with the work?'

'Yes Nurse.'

'It is a difficult time for her you know.'

'Yes Nurse.'

'She needs rest.'

'Yes Nurse.'

'Do you say your prayers every night?'

June did not answer and Lucille answered for her, 'No. She never says prayers, and I can't get her to Sunday school or mass. Cyrus neither. They are two heathens.'

Nurse soothed her. 'Never mind. Good things come to those who wait. She is saving up her faith for the future. That is all. June is not a heathen, are you June?' June did not answer and Nurse said. 'Come on, tell us you're not a heathen.'

'No Nurse.'

'You are a very good girl, June.'

June made a face and Nurse frowned and took a deep breath. 'Tell me about Ashook Rambarran at Lot No. 12.'

June became tense again and said nothing. She sensed that Nurse had decided to rebuke her and could think of no just reason for it. She sensed too a comparison was going to be made between she and Ashook.

Nurse asked, 'Do you think Ashook is a good boy?'

'I don't know, Nurse.'

'Well, I will tell you. No.' She paused. 'You went to St. Peter's with him. You remember he bullied you two years ago?'

'Yes Nurse.'

'What he did to you?'

'Stand at the door and block my way.'

'That was all he did to you? What else he did?'

'Threaten me.

'Tell me how he threatened you.'

'To beat me up.'

'Why?'

'If I din' give him my pencils.'

'And did you give him your pencils?'

'Yes Nurse.'

'Why did you give him your pencils? And don't keep on saying "Yes Nurse" and "No Nurse" when I just get you to stop. Go on, answer. Why did you give him your pencils?'

'Frightened.'

'You were afraid of him?'

'Yes.'

'Why were you afraid of him?'

43

'He would beat me up.

'How did you know he would beat you up?'

'He say so.'

'You believed he would beat you up?'

'Yes, Nurse.'

'But what gave you reason to think he would beat you up?' She told June not to answer yet, then went to the enamel bucket which was filled with boiled water, took the lid off and ladled out a cup of water, then helped herself to ice from the flask. She returned, tinkling the ice in the cup.

In the interval, all June's old anger with Ashook Rambarran returned and before Nurse had sat down again she began an outpouring. 'He told me if I didn't steal pencils for him he would beat me up, and I tell him I won' steal no pencils for him and I would tell my mother on him.'

Nurse gestured for her to stop. 'Yes. But you still *gave* him your pencils, and when you gave him all your pencils that left you no pencils to use. So how did you get new pencils? Did you borrow them?'.

'No.'

'Did you buy them?'

'No.'

'Where did you get them?'

June had genuinely forgotten and now she allowed Nurse to lead her to the past for the truth. It was coming back to her. 'From mother.'

'Did you ask mother first?'

'Yes.'

'What did you ask Mother?'

'Please could I have some more pencils.'

'And what did Mother say?'

'What happened to your pencils?'

'What did you tell her?'

'That I lose them.'

Nurse sighed, and relaxed on the couch again. June's tension was gone but her mind struggled with the burden of the truth. Her eyes met Nurse's and the questions in her mind raced around rapidly. Why did she let herself believe that

44

Ashook would beat her? Why did she tell a white lie to her mother? She was not really afraid of Ashook, so what was she really afraid of? Why did she let someone like Ashook frighten her when he was just a skinny, noisy boy? Before she could answer one question, another appeared in her mind, because they were simple questions with simple answers, and the simple answer to them all was that she did not think, she just reacted.

Nurse's eyes twinkled. 'A minute ago you told me you refused to steal pencils for Ashook.'

'Yes Nurse.'

'You told me you would not steal from your friends to give to him.'

'Yes Nurse.'

'Why? Because you liked your friends too much?'

'Yes Nurse.'

There was a long pause before Nurse spoke again. 'Do you think the way you got the pencils from Mother was a little like stealing?'

June did not take her eyes away from Nurse's. She answered 'Yes,' and then looked at Lucille who had stopped sewing and was looking from June to Nurse a little anxiously. After she said yes to Nurse, she wanted Lucille to be as surprised by the revelation as she was but Lucille was annoyed with Nurse and just turned away and began to undo some stitching. June's tension came back. It burned in her chest and lay like a clamp all over her body then soon produced the well of tears which she could not stop this time. She sobbed and Nurse took her in her arms and patted her back and rocked her, murmuring 'Awright my dear, awright.'

Lucille sighed and exclaimed 'Oh dear, oh dear,' over and over again.

When June had cried a good deal, Nurse laughed deeply and stood her on her feet. June wiped her eyes with her shirt.

'I always say a good cry is the best cure of all!' Nurse declared cheerfully. She shook her gently and told her to look her in the eyes again. Sniffing, June did as she was told. 'Now look here, June. You are a strong girl. You hear me? What did I just say?'

'That I am a strong girl, Nurse.'

'Good. Now I am a little puzzled here. You understood me very well. You know what is required. All the good things, my dear, all the good things that the Lord gives us, courage, strength, honesty, to strive and strive ever more to rise to our fullest moral power, my dear. We are not born strong. We are born weak, my dear. We *learn* strength and understanding, my dear. Now you are a child that knows that. Mother has taught it to you. Do you agree with me?'

'Yes Nurse.'

'So what is troubling you, my dear?'

'Nothing Nurse.'

Nurse turned and spoke to Lucille, 'Have you spoken to Cyrus? Does he have any idea what is bothering the child?'

'No,' Lucille replied.

'What does he suggest?'

'Nothing. He has a lot of work on, with the lavatory expenses and all the digging and building involved to pay for. And I feeling so sick. June has gone to the dogs this holiday, and with no bad company to influence her.'

Nurse reassured Lucille, 'June is a good girl.' She winked at June, 'No child of mine goes to the dogs. I brought her into this world, I delivered her, so I am bound to know. Tell me all the things you did this holiday, June.'

'Ride about,' June said.

'What else?'

'Play on the watertank.'

Lucille commented, 'I told her not to play on that watertank. It is empty and full of wet tar. She will fall in and only then will she listen to me. She is always climbing that guinep tree. She is a tomboy. She rips all her clothes on that tree.'

Nurse winked and asked June, 'What else you did?'

'Play school.'

Lucille complained, 'She has written all over that tank, on the outside, with chalk. She plays teacher.'

Nurse exclaimed, 'Oh good! Then you must be looking forward to starting school in New Amsterdam. You see, Lucille, the child can't wait to go to school.'

46

Lucille said, 'Not her, the school isn't good enough for her! Poor children would give their right arm to go to that school but not her.'

Nurse soothed Lucille, 'Hush Lucille, don't talk so bitter to the child.'

Lucille continued. 'We are paying seventy-five dollars a term.'

Nurse raised her eyebrows and spoke to June, 'One hundred dollars if you include the uniform and books this term, more if you had given the uniform to a New Amsterdam seamstress to sow.' Nurse kept her eyes on June as she spoke, then said to Lucille. 'It's the school, Lucille. June is anxious about the school.'

Lucille nodded. 'That is exactly what it is.'

'But she says she is looking forward to it too.

Lucille sighed. 'Well then it may be something else.'

'No, I think it is the school. It is a big change for her you know.'

'Well if she can't cope with it we had better not bother. It would be a waste of money to send her if she doesn't want to go.'

Nurse asked June, 'Tell me the truth, you want to go to New Amsterdam High School?'

June looked at Lucille who seemed not to care any more, and felt sorry for the trouble she had given her. She replied, 'Yes.'

Nurse told Lucille, 'You have your answer.'

Lucille woke June early. She told her that there would be no more time to lie in bed and daydream, that the journey to school would take a good hour of cycling.

There was excitement in Lucille's voice when she called again, 'Six o'clock now! You must leave at six-thirty to give yourself time to get there for eight o'clock.' She added a caution, 'If you see anything unusual on the road – Boysie and his men maybe, stirring up trouble round the factory, if it looks dangerous, get off the public road. Go to Savitri in the junior staff compound or come back home right away if the road is clear.'

June complained, 'What point there is going to school if the strike going close down estate. There will be no money to pay fees.'

Lucille replied, 'That's exactly the reason you have to get your education, because one day this plantation will shut down. There is no future here, no living for you.'

June crossed the public road to fill her bucket at the standpipe. The dirt road was no longer damp from the wetting it got every afternoon, especially in the dry season, to keep down the dust. Yesterday, she had helped with the wetting but the dust had already been disturbed by the lorries which took away the first exodus of workers. She was always half-awake at three o'clock when the women rose and began to cook and clean. Through the veil of sleep she would hear their voices, the sounds of cooking, and their trips to the standpipe. When the lorries came and took the workers away she would fall into a deep sleep for two hours before waking for school at seven o'clock, by which time the second exodus from the villages would begin. Most of the first exodus of workers were for the far-flung canefields, some for the factory; others were not plantation workers but workers in New Amsterdam and beyond who travelled on Ali's bus, some to change to Corentyne buses or the Rosignol ferry. At eight o'clock the children left for school, as she used to do. Now, she was going to be part of the second exodus.

The second exodus included the casual labourers who turned up at Old Dam high bridge where the overseers would allocate them work in the nearby canefields, the canals, the stables, the factory, the junior and senior staff compounds. It also included people who worked in New Amsterdam; the nurses, porters and clerks for the hospital, market hucksters, workers for the stores and workshops, servants and road workers. Many in the second exodus came from Lucius and Adelphi villages. These were no longer exclusively plantation villages; freed slaves had bought the land there and their families still kept the rights, and the custom of not working for the plantation. People who were able to make a living from the one or two acre farms which were now being leased by the Sugar Industry Labour Welfare Fund always moved to Lucius and Adelphi villages. It was a constant worry to Cyrus and Lucille that, one day, the overseers would ask them to move out of New Dam, which was still very much a plantation village, the first village of extra-nuclear cottages to be built by the estate. Cyrus always said that he would prefer to move to Adelphi to the south, closer to the forest, than to Lucius which lay to the north of New Dam.

'June! June!' Lucille was calling from the cottage. 'You are daydreaming again, you will be late!'

The bucket was overflowing at her feet. She lifted it out of the well and hurried across the road.

All her anxious feelings had to be forgotten during her preparations. Lucille was still ironing the pleats of her skirt, stopping often to call out instructions to her while she bathed in the wooden bathroom under the guinep tree: 'Use plenty of soap! Scrub your neck and knees! Rinse off all the soap!'

After her wash, she wrapped herself in her towel and ran across the yard, up the back stairs. Lucille dried her as if she were still a small child, fussing in a way she had long stopped doing. June felt as if she were being made a new person all over again, so hard had she scrubbed herself. Now Lucille was drying her as if to rub away more old skin, rubbing her hair and round her ears so briskly, her head hurt.

Her new uniform was laid out on the bed. All of it was new, even the belt, socks and underwear. Lucille had used new spools of thread to sew it. There was a new tin of talcum powder too. First, she was dusted heavily with the powder. When the perfume filled her nostrils June felt that it was like being prepared for church – the bathing, drying, powdering and dressing of yourself, like putting on a new skin that had to look, smell and fit better than your old one. Lucille would not put on the uniform until she had brushed June's hair, in case any fell on the white blouse. Her hair was brushed until it shone. The white blouse shone too, with a bluish sheen. There was not a crease in it. Lily-white socks, then her royal blue skirt went on, then the black leather shoes with brass buckles, then the bow-tie with the pair of tails and the black leather belt over her blouse. Lucille turned her round and round, inspecting her anxiously, then clipped her pen and pencil to her blouse. With her bicycle bag full of books and her saucepan of food they went downstairs together, to the bicycle which they had cleaned and serviced the day before. She had last cycled out of New Dam when she visited the Beardsleys. Now she felt the same worry which she had felt then. She told herself it was useless to worry. This taking leave of New Dam for another place and people was going to be a daily part of her life now. If she always let it affect her so badly what was going to become of her? Nothing could be worse than the visit to the Beardsleys, worse than their scorn for plantation workers.

Lucille stayed at the gate until June reached the bridge. Once past the bridge, the shrubs and trees hid her from view. June concentrated on enjoying the ride. There was a skill to cycling over the earth road. She knew the rough and smooth of it, where the earth was worn and the stones and pot-holes exposed. The sun was barely warm yet but she was already hot. She put on her Panama hat, pulling the elastic cord tight around her chin.

Beyond the Anglican church, the road was crowded with workers – women, boys and men. They sat in the grass along the parapets or stood in the road. The overseers were grouped at the high bridge. She recognised the people from New Dam among the workers and they raised a cutlass or pitchfork in greeting. At the bridge she jumped off and walked. This was the first time she had ever seen the overseers and workers together like this. At the top of the bridge, the downward slope was not as steep but fanned out on one side to form a hill. There, the overseers were in conference with the foremen who went back and forth distributing piecework from the overseers to the workers. The overseers did not speak directly with a worker. They turned their backs on them and spoke amongst themselves, pausing only to deal with a foreman. These were the field overseers – Overseer Sam Cameron, Vincent Chu, two Indian overseers, and others. Overseer Cameron was sitting astride his motorcycle, a cigar in his mouth, a sweaty hat on his head, his skin sunburnt. His wife, an Amerindian woman, sometimes rode her horse through New Dam. Unlike Overseer Cameron she was very small, a beautiful woman with long straight hair which fell to her waist. Her horse was a large brown and white roan which tossed its long mane as it cantered by. The Indian overseer was wearing the old fashioned cork hat, short trousers and knee length socks which were long out of date.

June cycled down the slope past the factory and bachelor compound, pedalled hard through the senior and junior staff compounds, past the Welfare Club which had been built with money from the Labour Welfare Fund. It was supposed to provide recreation for the workers but it was really a club for the junior staff only. There was a new, small library there which June had joined, and read most of the books already. Apart from the library, the club was really a cricket ground with two large pavilions and pitches that were in such good condition it was beginning to attract the Georgetown clubs. There was even talk about the English cricket team, the M.C.C., coming to play there.

Now she rode through Canefield Village, the largest plantation village in the whole of Canefields. It was twice the size of New Dam, and as well kept, because half of it contained the extra nuclear cottages which were meant to be proof that the sugar estates were looking after the welfare of their workers, and a way of persuading the workers that they should not follow Cheddi Jagan and defy the management. Villages like Pheasant, nearer the forest, were the smallest, given to flooding and erosion by the river.

She had crossed the bridge over Canefield canal and put New Dam well behind her when she saw Mariam Mootoo, a large basket balanced on her head. Mariam waved her to stop. June braked too quickly and her books slipped from the carrier and fell to the road. She jumped off the bicycle, set it on the stand and began to retrieve her books.

Mariam put down her basket, and took off the *kata,* the cloth-pad she used to rest it on, from her head. She dropped her cutlass and sack too and squatted to help June dust the books. She talked all the while in a mixture of Hindi and creolese, admiring the books. 'Eh eh, *bachcha* yuh tu'n *vidvan,* goin' to *madarsa! A* wan prappa nice *kitab* dis, man. *Aray bapray bahin,* now yuh mus' teach me fo' write *chitthi* an' use *kalam.'*

Mariam was teasing her, in the same way she liked to tease Lucille, whom she called 'mor', meaning peacock (she called Cyrus 'simn', meaning lion). Mariam used the word 'vidvan' meaning scholar instead of the word 'vidyarthini' which meant girl-student.

June packed her books and buckled them to the carrier again. Mariam watched her, murmuring on in Hindi. Now Mariam touched her shirt, murmuring 'kamij', then her pen, saying it was a nice 'kalam', then her skirt, commenting what a nice 'kapda' it was too.

'Well *bahin* tell y'u *badibahin* nuh? Y'u feelin' *santosh?'* Mariam gestured towards New Amsterdam. She was asking her if she felt happy to be going to New Amsterdam, the place where they did not like sugar plantation coolies. When June did not answer, Mariam asked whether she did not understand Hindi any longer.

'Only some words,' June replied.

'You use fo' talk Hindi! You *bap* too, but you ma don' 'low y'u now. Now y'u goin' town, now y'u gon talk prappa English!' Mariam nodded, threw her head back and laughed.

Lucille liked to say that Mariam was in love with Cyrus. Cyrus said it was not true. June could not imagine Cyrus married to Mariam, or Mariam as her mother. But Mariam was always stopping her at the roadside, wanting to have conversations with her, trying to behave as if she was her mother. Mariam gave June presents – rare and sweet waternuts which she brought from the creeks and canals in the distant canefields where she worked, and once she sat on a culvert with Mariam and shared her saucepan of roti, pumpkin curry and achar. She never told Lucille about it. Lucille said that Mariam was uncivilised and aggressive like Boysie. She was a casual labourer on the estate and had leased one of the new, small plots of land near the Welfare Club where she grew vegetables and ground provisions to sell at the market. Her father, Dhookie, was crippled – his right leg had been amputated after a snake bit him in the canefield. Her brother, Lakhan, was an alcoholic, and her other brother, Jack, suffered from epilepsy. Mariam was the breadwinner of the family.

Now Mariam was telling her that she should remember her Hindi. She spoke a whole sentence to June: *'Maim Hindi Sikhta hum,'* and asked if she understood it. When June shook her head, Mariam threw up her hands in despair and exclaimed, *'Aray bapray!'* Then she reached into her bosom where she kept her money, drew out a knotted handkerchief, opened it and handed her a gill. June shook her head. Mariam insisted, *'Paisa!'*

'No,' June said. 'I can't take it. I got money.' She took the dollar bill which Lucille had given her from her pocket and showed it to Mariam.

Mariam's face fell. She wrapped up her coins again and replaced them in her bosom, then she reached into the fold of her headkerchief and took out a few crumpled bills. She offered June a two-dollar bill. June shook her head again. Mariam sighed and replaced the bills. June felt sorry now that she had not taken the money. Mariam had never married and had children like most Indian women. She was one of the most good-looking and hard-working of them. Her dark skin was smooth, her long neck graceful. Though her hair was rough from exposure, her hairline framed her face attractively and her hair was swept up under her headkerchief. The men liked her, and the women were jealous of her. She had what they liked to call a good figure. Lucille did praise Mariam once for what she called her 'carriage' and told June that she should learn to push back her shoulders, hold in her stomach and walk erect like Mariam, but Lucille also said that it was sheer hard labour, the long walk to the backdam, the bailing of punts and swinging of the cutlass, not breeding, which gave Mariam such a good figure and carriage. Lucille herself was short and plump.

Now Mariam recited in Hindi, the maxims which June should follow. Nani Dharamdai was also fond of reciting these to her. They were the Hindi sentences which she did remember: *'Saph kapde pahano, bhagvan ki prarthana karo, apra path padho, kam khao, badom ka adar karo, kisi ki ninda mat karo, sab ko pyar karo, jor se mat bolo, apna kam khiia karo.'*

June helped lift Mariam's basket to her head, handed her the sack and cutlass, then took her leave, hopping on the pedals a few times before jumping on.

'Meri bat suno!' Mariam called after her.

In Lucius Village, there was a steady traffic of cyclists and pedestrians on the public road. Students had begun to appear in Canefields. The older girls wore the uniform of New Amsterdam High School. Some wore the uniform of the two other schools. The boys all wore khaki trousers, white shirts and different ties. They rode in pairs or singly. Hire cars also appeared in Canefields. They were parked where the asphalted road began and continued all the way to New Amsterdam. When people appeared along one of the paths the drivers would hoot the horns and harangue them to join their car. The servants, in their white and green uniforms, were walking all the way. A few donkey carts cantered along, their lanterns swaying at the rear. Mitch, who was the only taxi driver in New Dam, sat on a culvert beside his car. He was drinking from a hot flask. He waved his cup and called out a greeting:

'You going to school, you going to school!'

She called back, 'Yes!'

'Walk good, walk good!'

The road was worst in Cumberland Village, so bad that June had to dismount several times. Cumberland had a village council and there was disagreement between New Amsterdam Town Council and New Dam estate management about their responsibilities for Cumberland. Few plantation workers lived there though the canals, backdam and the public road were used heavily by the estate, and there were canefields to the east and west of the village. Neglect showed in congested drains and bushy trees. June often heard talk about the old 'nigger yards' of Cumberland, a village which had never housed indentured Indians, though since that time the Africans had sold many of their lots to Indians. The villagers wanted to be run by New Amsterdam, with the estate paying for use of the roads and backdam, but the dispute remained unsettled while every morning the exodus of workers to New Amsterdam continued. Boysie always used Cumberland as an example to prove to Mr. Easen that village councils only gave the overseers as well as the government an excuse to do nothing but exploit people. Mr. Easen always countered by saying that every village in rural Guiana was different depending on their history; some were purely African; some had only known indentureship, and those were the newest villages, like New Dam; and some like villages on the Corentyne had something like village councils but were run by powerful families which exploited their own poor as badly as the estates. It was up to each village to work out its own character, Mr. Easen said.

Cumberland ended at the junction with Sheet Anchor village to the west and Palmyra village to the east. All traffic met at the junction and became congested in Sheet Anchor. Cyrus had warned her to be careful here, as she got closer to New Amsterdam. Ali's blue bus, with the name *Madonna* painted on the side, was parked between four green Corentyne buses which bore the names: *Sinbad, Maharajah, Sheikh of Araby* and *Zorro*. The drivers shouted abuse at each other while

55

the porters clambered up the ladders at the rear of the buses and loaded the wooden holds with bicycles, crates, sacks and baskets which the hucksters and other passengers hoisted up to them. Ali was swearing at his porter, complaining bitterly that the police would fine him for overloading. When all the buses were loaded with passengers and goods they revved their engines and raced each other to the Dolphin swing-bridge.

Sheet Anchor was a fishing village. Black nets hung drying in the yards, some spread out on upturned boats, others along the windows and landings of the cottages where men and women worked at repairing them. The smell of the river greeted her as she neared the swing-bridge and the horizon cleared. The light was always different near the river, sending off reflections from the water to the surrounding land. There were more boats nearer the river; they lined the yards and the public road. Men and boys were busy round them; new boats being built, old boats being tarred and repaired. Women with large baskets of fish on their heads were making their way from the river towards the market at the junction where the roads from Canefields, Corentyne and New Amsterdam met.

The swing-bridge straddled the river like a pair of wide metal arms. The walls were made of iron and the slopes and platform were a skeleton of greenheart logs and iron coated thickly with tar and asphalt. The traffic choked to a halt on the upward slope and pandemonium reigned briefly as draycarts, pedestrians, cyclists, cars, buses and trucks jostled for space to cross the water, abuse loud in the air. Vehicles grazed pedestrians and cyclists, but it was a daily, well-rehearsed ritual. The women hucksters were the calmest and June walked among them, learning to pick her way by following their footing. The asphalt surface was worn in many places and the ravaged greenheart and rusty iron rafters gaped open to reveal the surface of the Canje River underfoot. The river was polluted here, the surface clouded with mud, litter, and dead fish used for bait floated in it. It was not like the river in the interior near the furthest Canefields villages which was wild, untamed and uncharted. They said that some of the interior creeks were so clean it was possible to drink the water. She felt a long way from home just looking at the river here. She followed the example of the others on the downward slope, mounting her bicycle again and letting it take her at speed down the slope, passing the draycarts and pedestrians, the breeze whipping her hat off and making it dance round her shoulders on the elastic band.

As she took the very wide bend a new landscape unfolded: New Amsterdam on the near horizon. The land billowed out all around her – a coconut grove filling the sky to her right, followed by the buildings of the mental hospital which Lucille had pointed out once on one of their shopping trips a long time ago. There were expanses of shrubland and two cricket fields around the hospital. A queue of inmates from the hospital were leaving the gates there, a uniformed warden leading the way. The land to her left was farmed by these inmates and prisoners from the New Amsterdam Jail which was also nearby; she had overheard Cyrus and Lucille talking about it. The whole area was a patchwork of allotments, with coconut trees breaking up the skyline and wooden huts and fences marking out boundaries here and there. The breeze was at its strongest here, where the land was open and exposed, a change from the congested villages through which she had cycled.

There was a second bend to take before the houses and the buildings of New Amsterdam High School, which bordered the town, were in full view. As she rounded the bend she saw Lavender Jones among the pedestrians. Lavender had walked from Lucius Village. June stopped to walk with her.

'This is a really nice bike,' Lavender commented.

June asked, 'Where your books?'

Lavender shrugged. 'I don' have none yet. My mother said I must ask if they have any second-hand.' She took a twenty dollar bill from her skirt pocket and showed it to June. 'She give me money to buy books.'

'You could borrow my own if you don't get any.'

'O.K.' Lavender pointed, 'Look, New Amsterdam High School.'

June told Lavender to sit on the carrier, she would tow her the rest of the way. Lavender took the books from the carrier,

June hopped on to the bicycle and when she was seated Lavender took a short run and hopped on to the carrier. They completed the journey together.

6 NEW WORLD

The buses were parked outside the school gate. June and Lavender joined the queue and crossed the bridge between the public road and the tall hedge which concealed the school. They found themselves standing in a compound of six large wooden buildings. In the centre of the compound was an open space of lawns, divided by a network of concrete paths. Only two of the buildings boasted glass windows, new wood with a fresh coat of white paint and new zinc roofs painted in green. The others were dilapidated, the maroon zinc roofs rusting, cladding weather-beaten. Yet with repairs and a fresh coat of paint, the old colonial shutters, brick pillars and ornamental balustrades and gables would have shown up the plainness of the new buildings. The compound was enclosed by tall hedges on the north and south and by old royal palms on the west. On the eastern side a dusty red street separated the compound from the sports field.

It was the country children who were entering through the narrow bridge between the hedges. The children from New Amsterdam were streaming into the compound through the tall old wooden archway between the royal palms. Most came on foot and on bicycles through that entrance, but there were also cars pulling up on the dusty street near the sports field, bringing more students.

June and Lavender exchanged anxious looks, June gripping the handlebars of the bicycle, her Panama hat draped from her neck, Lavender clutching the books. There were younger children and older children, and children of all the races and mixtures of the races. Canefields was a mixture of Afro and Indo-Guyanese with some villages having more of one than the other. New Dam was mostly Indo-Guyanese and Lucius was mostly Afro-Guyanese but all the villages were united by

59

their poverty, with only the saw mill and rice mill owners really well off, like overseers, able to employ people, although everyone said they were nowhere as rich as local people in other parts of Guiana. The other races and other mixtures were so few in Canefields they were rare. Not here. There were many European mixtures – Lucille called them 'coloured', many European children too, some perhaps Portuguese, and several Chinese children. June's only previous contact with other Chinese children had come on the rare occasions she had gone shopping with Lucille in New Amsterdam. All these children looked at home here. They laughed and talked and played freely, looked healthier, bigger and taller than the country children. She noticed especially how the Indian girls among them looked freer, some with their hair cut short (Lucille called this style the 'bob'). If they wore their hair long, it was not plaited into the flat tail of the country girls but worn in the American ponytail style, tied near the crown with a fancy ribbon, dancing loose to their shoulders. They all looked more at ease in the high collars, ties, socks and leather shoes than June felt. She was used to going barefoot or wearing canvass shoes to primary school. She had had only one pair of leather shoes in her life, shoes for church, and she had worn them only three times. These children spoke the most practised English she had ever heard, not bothering with shaping the vowels carefully like Lucille, but letting the words slide over their tongues. They came and went past her and Lavender like people from another world.

A yellow bus now drew up at the gate. The words 'New Dam Pln.' were painted on the side. Apart from one Indian and one African boy, both of whom looked to be sixteen or so, all the children who got off the bus were nearer June's age, starting school. Lucille had said that the children of the overseers always went to boarding schools in England when they reached secondary school age but sometimes attended local school for a year or two first. There were only two European children in the group though – Annie Beardsley and a red-haired, freckle-faced boy. They crossed the bridge with an African girl, and an Indian boy and girl.

Annie Beardsley did not look around the school at all. She kept her eyes on the ground. She looked uncomfortable in her uniform. Seeing Annie in the uniform, June realised how much she disliked it. It was too self-important, with the ridiculous bow-tie with the pair of tails, the blouse having to be worn over the skirt then tied with a belt. The bow was something like the collar of the magistrate when he came to the court in Canefields. You only dressed up like this when you wanted to puff yourself out for church, or if you were a policeman, lawyer, priest or hospital matron. Annie looked reluctant to be important in the uniform. That, and her sickly appearance, attracted attention though she stayed close to her group. Another plantation bus arrived, this one from the Corentyne, and dropped off a larger group of European children. They joined the New Dam group of plantation children, and some of the European children from New Amsterdam greeted them.

Now a bell rang out from the large building nearest the playing fields and the children began to drift towards this building. The new pupils stayed near the gates, scattered thinly round the lawn, and June saw for the first time that there seemed to be many country children among the first year students, more than there seemed to be among the older students, and the new country students numbered as many Indians as Africans. Soon four teachers appeared along one of the paths – three women and one man. They lined up in a row before the new pupils and the oldest of the women began to speak.

'Good morning, students. My name is Mrs. Farley. I am very glad to see you all. I am not going to make a speech now. All the speeches are going to be made in the auditorium.' She pointed to the building the children were still entering in a long queue. Now June noticed Mrs. Farley's cane. She was using it to point to the auditorium. None of the other teachers carried canes. Mrs. Farley continued, 'I have here a list of names for forms one, two and three.' The list was handed to her by the male teacher. She pointed her cane at one of the teachers, who was standing a few feet away. 'Mr. Doodnauth is form teacher for Form One, Miss Lewis is form teacher for Form Two, and Mrs. Adams for Form Three. Now I will first call the names of students who have been put in Form One, and as I call your names you are to line up in front of Mr. Doodnauth who will then lead you off to the auditorium. I will do likewise for Forms Two and Three and you will take your respective places in front of your respective teachers. Do you understand me?' Some of the students nodded. Mrs. Farley's face turned from serious to severe quickly. She demanded, 'I beg your pardon?', and asked again, her voice rising, 'Do you understand me?'

Murmurs of 'Yes Miss,' rose sluggishly from the group. Mrs. Farley shook her cane at them. 'I will have to teach you all manners. When I speak to you, especially when I ask a question, I expect you all to speak up very loudly. Now I will ask again and you had all better be in good voice. I love to use this cane. Now I will ask again. Do-you-understand-me?'

There was a loud chorus, 'Yes Miss!'

June and Lavender had not spoken, and June looked around and saw how nervous everyone looked. Mrs. Farley began to read off the names on the list and they began to line up in front of their form teachers.

To June, this was a disaster. She tried to remember her recent ordeal at the Beardsleys and told herself nothing could be worse than that, but the thought of being whipped by Mrs. Farley made her flesh feel very vulnerable. She had been lucky at primary school to have had the kindest teachers, like Mrs. Lawrence in the preparatory class who picked the lice from their hair, bought a special shampoo with her own money and liked to visit their homes and meet their parents, who never raised her voice or abused anyone. In her next year there was Mrs. Harris who was pregnant that year and did not like to whip, while nearby in Mr. Singh's and Mrs. Bancroft's classes, the whip flew round, stinging the flesh of the children like wild marabuntas let loose on them, the sight hypnotising June into applying herself to her work and doing well enough not to be whipped – the only guarantee against caning. The next year, in Second Standard, they were given a young teacher who did not like using the cane. Again she was lucky, while in the lower grade Second Standard classes, the whip flew around freely, wreaking havoc, turning young children into nervous cases. Parents who did not like it withdrew their children from the school, feeling they would have a more useful life at home or at work. June was barely able to stay ahead in that embattled atmosphere and avoid the 'dunce' classes. In the third and fourth standard she was not so lucky. Mr. Richards spared the bright ones, she among them, but whipped everyone else freely. However, it was her most harrowing year at primary school because Mr. Richards did not spare anyone his threats and sarcasm. He was the first person she ever really disliked, a conceited man with the build of a boxer. He spoke perfect English and was abusive with it, even to those he liked to call his favourites. In the fourth standard, Mrs. Grace was just like Mr. Richards, though the torture she practised was more refined. She liked to stand over a pupil and point the tip of the cane into the neck for several minutes as they struggled with an essay or an arithmetic problem. In preparation for a caning she would first take her handkerchief from her bosom, wipe her face, neck and hands, then blow her nose, then smooth her hair, straighten her clothing, then position her victim carefully into a corner from which there was no escape, reposition them carefully again after the delivery of each lash, pausing in between to catch her breath. June played harder than ever that year. Through play you were able to live down these stresses but as you got older it became harder to play and you became more, not less, prey to them. Her last year at primary school was the best of all, erasing the memories of the bad things of the years before. It was the year when Mr. Sam taught her. He loved learning and teaching with a love for sharing which turned it into inspiration for everyone. Only Mrs. Lawrence and Mr. Sam could make each child in a class bloom with confidence, or heal them.

Here at New Amsterdam High School each child was important because their parents paid fees. The uniform was a badge of privilege bought for you by your parents. You brought disgrace on it if you showed feelings of worry, doubt or fear. Playing like a child would not be an answer here, it would be a sign of backwardness. If you were whipped here you would have to learn to bear it as if you were made of steel. This made the spectre of Mrs. Farley's cane more terrifying, more destructive.

Now Mrs. Farley was reading out their names; Lavender's name came before June's and they became separated, but they were in the same form, Form Two; so was Annie Beardsley. Their teacher was the youngest of the teachers, Miss Lewis. She led them to the auditorium.

The whole school was gathered in the auditorium, the youngest children in the front rows, the older children at the back. They were like a young army, all the girls dressed the same, all the boys in the school tie, khaki trousers and white shirts. The teachers sat in a row on the platform, the headmaster standing at the lectern, some teachers stood in the aisle. Mrs. Farley led them to the empty rows of chairs in the middle of the auditorium and signalled for them to file past her into their seats. As they filed past she slapped the slower children briskly on the shoulder. June found herself among the victims. The slap burnt like shame on her shoulder, then anger made her heart race. She kept her eyes on the floor, thinking that the whole school had seen her disgrace. When they were all seated she lifted her eyes and looked for Lavender who was sitting at the end of the row, with Mrs. Farley standing beside her. They exchanged anxious looks again.

Although the headmaster was Indian and Mrs. Farley was African, they looked alike: hair streaked with grey, thick spectacles, lips twisted into a pout, large front teeth. They looked down scornfully at everyone and everything around them, their look changing from disgust to anger in turn. Now, the headmaster spoke. He welcomed the new students and introduced himself, Mr. Singh. He asked for hymn books to be given to the new students. When this was done he led the singing of 'All creatures that on earth do dwell.' When the hymn was over Mr. Singh read from the bible. After this everyone sat and Mr. Singh made a serious speech to the new students. He told them that they were very privileged to come to New Amsterdam High School. It was the oldest school in the county, and many sons and daughters of British Guiana had been educated here. He mentioned a few names, which were not that many, but he said that one of these would soon become a member of the legislative assembly in Georgetown. They had a grave responsibility to maintain a tradition of high professional achievement. How could they, the new students, follow in the footsteps of those great men and women who had gone before? He paused for a minute or two and June could hear the noise of the traffic outside – engines going at speed along the highway as they raced along the breeze-lashed stretch which connected the swingbridge to New Amsterdam. She could hear the hooves of a horse going at speed too, and the wheels of the draycart it was pulling. All day long peasant farmers and fishermen and women walked to and from New Amsterdam along that stretch of highway – the great expanse of space which separated the town from the villages. In the villages you worked and struggled to eat and stay alive. Here in New Amsterdam you were assured of food and work, you did not have to concentrate your energies on finding either. You had to concentrate your energies on becoming great men and women and keeping up the fine traditions of New Amsterdam High School. But the life of the villages was there outside, at the junction where business between town and country was going on – food being brought into New Amsterdam, labourers being brought in to do the work the great men and women did not do. The loud horn of a country bus sounded and she turned and looked outside, through the wide windows to see Ali's bus, *Madonna* racing a Corentyne bus towards the swingbridge. The hold on top of the bus was loaded with bicycles, baskets, crates and oil drums.

Mr. Singh was now telling them how to achieve their ambitions – hard work, he said, hard dedicated work. He made it sound like punishment. There would be punishment for failure, he promised. Failure was not going to be tolerated.

Laggards and idlers were not welcome in this school. He pointed in the direction of the mental hospital, then in the opposite direction, towards the jail. Those were the correct places for laggards and idlers, he said, not here. Only decent people came to New Amsterdam High School. If you were not decent you had better start thinking of going somewhere else, of taking up street cleaning or canecutting but don't confuse yourself with the fine people who this school had produced if you had no intention of working hard. He spoke as if labourers did not work hard, were labourers because they were laggards and idlers. She thought of her friends from primary school who were brighter than she was but too poor to be able to afford to come to this school.

Mr. Singh's temper grew the more he excited himself with his hatred of inferiority, but he controlled himself eventually and brought his tirade to an end. He took a deep breath and asked them to rise and sing 'There is a green hill far away.' They sang without the grief they sang with at the Anglican church in Old Dam, where they sang in a bittersweet way as if to console themselves, as if they did not really believe that their hymns reached God, or even that God existed, but sang them anyway. They sang here almost as if they were boasting they were Christians. The next hymn was 'Onward Christian Soldiers'. At the back of the auditorium someone stamped his feet in time.

Mr. Singh spoke again. He welcomed new teachers, asked the assembly to pray for two teachers who were ill, and announced the forthcoming retirement of another. He spoke about last year's examination results. They were the best in the county of Berbice but they were not as good as the best schools in Georgetown. He would not rest until they matched the performance of the students in those schools. New Amsterdam High School had produced one Guiana Scholar who had completed his 'O' levels before going to school in Georgetown to do his 'A' levels. He turned to the teachers behind him and demanded to know when they would give him a Guiana Scholarship. He warned this year's sixth formers that they were in for a very hard time this year – he would be keeping a close, personal eye on them. After this, he summarised last years sports achievements and outlined the next year's programme. Then he spoke for a long time about the public image of the students. There were those who constantly disgraced their uniform in public – those who seemed to think they could conduct courtships in broad daylight, in their uniforms;

there were those who liked to idle outside cakeshops and rumshops in the company of vagrants; there were even those who used obscene language in public, language fit only for the 'pit' section in the cinema, indeed students in uniform were often seen in the pit at the cinema. Let those who wished to come to this school speak a language which brought honour on their uniform and conduct themselves like future leaders and superior citizens of this country. Mr. Singh promised that he would keep a close eye on the inferior students in and outside the school; he would make it his duty to confront them in public; his duty to the school was paramount; it was a matter of honour which he lived with night and day, in and outside the school, and he expected everyone, teachers and students, to follow his example. Would you believe it, he asked – he had received complaints from the residents of New Amsterdam about the behaviour of students. He listed the complaints: stealing from fruit trees, rudeness, smoking, drinking, trespassing, molesting of women and girls, and other nuisances. The culprits were known, their names were on a blacklist, they would be expelled after four warnings – that was all to be said about it. When this speech was over they sang another hymn June did not know, then the new students were asked to lead the way out of the auditorium. Mrs. Farley signalled them to follow her.

Mrs. Farley led them to the newest building in the compound. They marched behind her in a single line along a crumbling concrete path which was separated from a tennis court by a tall, worn wire fence. The bottom storey bore a sign: Science Laboratory. Mrs. Farley led them up the long flight of stairs into a long empty room which was divided into two by one of the two blackboards there. Only the blackboard separated the desks and chairs which were arranged for two classes. Mrs. Farley instructed Form Two to occupy the classroom nearest the door. She sent Form Three down the stairs again, round the building, to the rear stairs which led to their own entrance. June was glad when Miss Lewis arrived to take over from Mrs. Farley.

Miss Lewis spoke. Her voice was so timid and nervous the students felt relief – they began to talk and laugh freely. Miss Lewis raised her voice, but not sharply – it took a lot of effort out of her.

'Now look here, it's not polite to speak while I am speaking.' Miss Lewis insisted.

This silenced them only for a few seconds. Miss Lewis looked helpless and angry. She ordered them to be silent but they ignored her. Desperate, she began to explain their first year work. She tried to be heard above the talk and laughter, raising a book now and then to illustrate her talk. Now she described the timetable and copied it on the blackboard. No one was taking any notice.

Form Two was divided into two sections, with four rows of five or four desks on either side of the aisle. At the back of the right row sat four of the Plantation children, with Lavender at the end of the row, next to Annie Beardsley. June had found herself in the second row on the right, an Indian girl on her left, an African girl on her right. They were mostly Afro and Indo-Guyanese boys and girls. A group of Indian boys and one African boy filled the two back rows in her section. In front of the plantation children sat three boys – two Indians and one African – and a European girl. The front row of that section was filled by an African and Indian boy, one European boy and an Indian girl. All the girls in the row in front of June were Indian girls – she was sure they were from the country, because of their hairstyle, the flat, plaited tails, and because they looked as nervous as she and Lavender. Their speech was not Canefields or New Amsterdam. Perhaps they were from the West Coast. She sensed that the girls in her row and the row behind, were from New Amsterdam – the row behind was the noisiest, followed by the boys behind who spoke unashamedly and cheerfully in their country accents.

Now Miss Lewis took the register. She warned them that if they did not answer to their names she would mark them absent. They quietened down then.

'Fazia Bacchus, Rita Bachan, Annie Beardsley...'

There was no 'Here Miss' from Annie. Miss Lewis repeated her name. All their eyes followed the eyes of the plantation children to rest on Annie who was staring blankly at her desk.

'Annie Beardsley?' Miss Lewis repeated.

There were sniggers from the class.

'Annie Beardsley. Is Annie Beardsley absent or present?' Miss Lewis demanded.

The European boy in the back row stood up and said, 'She is present, Miss.' He pointed to Annie.

Miss Lewis frowned. 'Can she not speak for herself?'

The boy shook his head. Miss Lewis frowned deeper, wrote in the register and told him to sit.

'Celia Cato, Paula Duncan, Mahadai Gopaul...'

June noticed that the register was not divided between Indian and Christian names here, but between boys and girls. Mahadai Gopaul's name was repeated.

The girl directly behind June laughed and mimicked

'Mahadai Gopaul' in an exaggerated country accent: 'Ai gal Mahadai ah wha' y'u ah do gal, beti, Mahadai.' Then she changed to her own voice and declared that the name sounded like 'mad eye'.

Someone laughed loudly at this – the Indian boy in the row in front of the plantation children.

Mahadai Gopaul was sitting in front of June. Now she swung round and stared fiercely at the girl who had laughed at her name. This made them laugh even more. The laughter spread round the class until some of the country Indians were laughing at themselves too. No one laughed at the Indians whose names were half Christian, half Indian: names which belonged to those who were from New Amsterdam.

'Tina Jaikarran, Lavender Jones, Beverly Khan, Uma Khanhai,' (at this name they began to mimic the Hindu prayer, making mooing noises: 'Oom, oom, oom'), 'Lily Kissoon, June Lehall,' (at her name someone brayed over and over like a donkey: 'Hee haw, hee haw,' and they rocked with laughter), 'Sarojini Matadin,' (this drew laughter and more mimicry of country accents), 'Andrea Persaud, Kursati Ramotar,' (the laughter was becoming more not less excited), 'Yvonne Ramsammy, Cynthia Simmonds.'

The laughter which followed Cynthia Simmonds' response to her name was even more aggressive than the laughter at the country Indians. Cynthia Simmonds was one of the European children who had arrived on the Corentyne plantation bus. She was very plump, with straight blonde hair and very red cheeks. She had the look of a 'tomboy', a name June did not like because Lucille liked to use it about her. All through the anarchy Cynthia Simmonds had looked as if she were enjoying herself very much, her mouth full of gum which she chewed at busily, her blue eyes merry. It was Cynthia's voice that they were finding so funny. They did not have to mock it because Cynthia sounded as if she were mocking it herself, her English accent was so pronounced, (this was Lucille's word for an accent like this – an Anglican priest used to have an accent like this and Lucille would laugh and imitate it when she remembered him). If you put a large guinep in your mouth

70

and tried to speak you would sound like Cynthia Simmonds. They laughed for the longest time at her until she looked unhappy and her skin became red all over.

There was so much scorn in the class, June felt more anxious than ever. The country villages were targets of scorn here too, as they were to the overseers and their children, children like Sarah Beardsley.

Miss Lewis could not keep order, and it became worse when she called the names of the country boys. Yet, however much their names were laughed at, most of the country boys kept very serious faces and just looked coolly at the trouble-makers, as if daring them to laugh. The boy whose name excited the most laughter, Dhirendranauth Triveni, gave them all a cool, superior look. The name Triveni was a good Sanskrit name – Nani had told her so, it was a name to be proud of. Rabindranauth Motilall, though, joined the laughter at his own expense and laughed hardest when they called him 'Rotilall'. They called Prakash Mungroo 'Jackass Mongoose' and he laughed too.

June felt sick with disgust. It was not as if they laughed once, but all the time. Having an Indian name gave endless cause for abuse. It came as a shock to her that it was the town Indians who led the mockery, especially the three girls in the row behind her: Lily Kissoon, Rita Bachan and Beverly Khan, the girls with Christian first names.

Miss Lewis had become hoarse now, shouting to try and calm the disorder which taking the register had unleashed. In Form One next door Mr. Doodnauth was doing better. His students turned around and raised their eyebrows at Form Two. Miss Lewis announced that she was leaving now, and a Mrs. Baxter would arrive soon to explain the Maths for the year. As soon as she disappeared through the front door, their voices rose again.

One of the girls behind June declared, 'She's a teacher? I could teach!' When she caught June looking at her she stuck her tongue out at her and snapped, 'Don't stare at me, you!'

June snapped back, 'You can't tell me what to do!'

'Put her in her place, Rita!' one of her friends encouraged.

71

Rita put her fingers to her eyes and pulled them upwards into thin slits. 'Chinky chinee!' This brought down scornful laughter on June's head.

June turned away, her heart pounding with rage. She told herself to ignore it, to be cool and calm and let them think it did not trouble her at all, so that they would not get anything out of it, but her sense of injustice, not just for herself, had grown into anger and helplessness. She could not let it be, she turned around again and declared: 'I am Indian too!' daring them to laugh at her because she was from the country. They laughed until their eyes watered. She longed to get hold of Rita Bachan and pinch and cuff and choke her until she begged for mercy, to hurt her as much as she was hurting other people, to teach her a lesson. Rita Bachan draped her long hair across her shoulder and began to stroke it vainly. Did Rita think she was saying she was one of them, like them, a town Indian, not a country Indian? She touched her own hair. It was cut short, in the 'bob', like a boy's. No, she was not Indian like them, not the country girls, or the town girls, not what they called 'pure' Indian. This was what Rita Bachan was telling her, by stroking and showing off her long, clean, bushy pony tail.

The school was changing. The first forms were larger and numbered more African and Indian students than the sixth, fifth and fourth forms where more 'light-skinned' students were to be seen. Higher education for Africans and Indians was still a novelty but their chances for getting it were better now. Here in June's class, groups which usually had limited contact with each other were in close contact for the first time and they were testing each other roughly to see who was strongest, who weakest.

Now Lavender was shouting from the back of the class:

'Coolie! Coolie water rice!' She was shouting at the boys who were sitting in the opposite row.

One of the boys shouted back at Lavender: 'Pork-eater! Black Pudding Lady!'

It was getting worse by the minute. One by one, they were sucked in, throwing around every racial abuse they knew,

72

everyone becoming a victim.

Now Lily Kissoon reached across and poked June in the back. 'What is your name again?' June did not answer or turn around. 'You don't have a voice?' June was determined not to give her any cause to abuse her.

Rita Bachan whispered, 'Lehall, her name is Lehall or something like that.'

'Oi! Something-Like-That, you don' have a tongue? You can't speak? Speak when you're spoken to. Country Bacoo!' Lily Kissoon persisted.

This did not raise any laughter until Rita caught sight of the saucepan at June's feet, held her nose, pointed at it and shouted, 'Look! Coolie saucepan! Smell the food! You all ever smell coolie saucepan? It stink of curry!'

The girls in Rita's row held their noses and pretended to choke on the smell and got a lot of laughs for their antics. The country girls in the front row looked at June and the saucepan with pity. For all her preparations, her effort to make June look like a town girl, Lucille had made two mistakes which marked June out – the saucepan of food which none of the other country girls had brought, and the books which June carried. Lucille had forgotten that the first day of school was a half-day, that lunch and books were not necessary.

Carried away by her success, Rita continued to try and raise more laughs. She began to mimic Mrs. Farley. She went to the front of the class, screwed up her lips and eyes and pretended to be brandishing a cane. Then she walked up and down the aisle, slapping students on the shoulder and barking out, 'You think you're here to have a holiday? I will show you, I will cane you good and proper, lazy good-for-nothings! So you all want to come to a good high school like this? I will show you, I will show you you don't deserve to be here!' Everyone laughed. When footsteps sounded on the stairs Rita rushed back to her seat and the class quietened down. They were afraid of Mrs. Farley, they feared she was returning.

A tall, beautiful woman entered the classroom. She walked straight in without glancing at them. Her hair was straightened and swept up in a bun near the crown of her head. With her long, bare neck and elegant walk she seemed to float along the aisle. She wore the kind of dress that was the latest craze, according to Lucille, the 'tent'. June had seen photographs of it in one of Lucille's old catalogues. The dress was made of yards of pretty flowered cloth and flowed out at the back and front from the small round collar and sleeveless shoulders. This was Mrs. Baxter, June guessed. Still not looking at them, she straightened the teacher's desk and chair, sat down, spread out her books and papers carefully, planted her elbows on the desk, checking the spot where she planted them as if to make sure it was not dirty, then placed her chin carefully on her fingers. All these studied gestures hypnotised the children. At last, she looked at them. Her look was a stare.

'My name is Mrs. Baxter, I am going to teach you mathematics this year. Now you have all come from many different schools. In the past we only took children from New Amsterdam schools but more of you country children have entered the school than ever before. This causes great difficulty with getting through the syllabus. Now, tell me, how many of you got beyond ratios at your schools?' Her voice was not timid like Miss Lewis's voice. It was clear and confident as a bell. But her voice soon became irritable, like Mrs. Farley's, when she learnt that the country children did not know ratios. Mrs. Baxter turned her look on June, and asked her, 'Why is it you have not done ratios?'

June wondered why it was that Mrs. Farley and now Mrs. Baxter picked on her. Her voice came out in a croak, her throat was so dry. 'My teacher asked me to explain to you he could not finish work in fractions and go on to ratios. He said I must say he is sorry.'

Lily Kissoon and Rita Bachan were giggling behind her back; they were mimicking her accent.

Mrs. Baxter sighed, and went on to question each student in turn, not smiling once, her beautiful black eyes icy and hard when she became displeased. In the end, she declared, 'Well those of you who are behind will just have to do your best to catch up. I will give one lesson in ratios, one only...' June looked away to avoid Mrs. Baxter's accusing eyes, '...and you

74

had better take it in. Then I will go straight into algebra. I am not going to tolerate any laziness at all. When I set work you do it, if you don't do it, that is your lookout.'

The next teacher was Tyrone Sylvester. He walked breezily into the classroom, chatted cheerfully with Mrs. Baxter, then sat on the desk when she left.

He greeted them playfully, 'Good morning, good morning, spring chickens!' Good humour seemed to surround him – the way he sat on the desk, his untidy curly hair, his paunch, the way he pinched and played with the chalk between his fingers, and the impish expression on his face – he was lively without being nervous or anxious, lively and looking for a lively response around him. June could hear the whispers of Lily Kissoon and Rita Bachan from behind – they were whispering that they knew Mr. Sylvester, he was a 'douglah', a drunk, he was engaged to be married to someone they knew, he lived in Winkle, he had been to school in Georgetown, at Queen's College. The way they talked, they seemed to feel they were superior to him. Mr. Sylvester noticed their whispering and quipped, 'Penny for your thoughts?' He waited for their response and when there was none continued to speak, 'So you have all come to secondary school? Second to what I wonder?' This made them laugh. 'You know, I don't like this idea that as we go through our education, it gets harder, more difficult, that we move from a lower to a higher plane. You see, education is not like that at all, my dears...' When their amusement at being called 'my dears' died down he continued. 'But secondary school it is. Well it's second to primary school, isn't it. At primary school you learnt to read and write and use numbers, and all the time, as you go through and reach fifth standard, you pick up all the bits and pieces of learning which you are going to continue here, you know, in the guise of new subjects like Biology, Algebra, Geometry, Chemistry, Physics etc. etc. Don't be frightened of these big new names. You did Nature Studies and General Science and these were the foundation for the subjects you will study here so you have not landed in space m'dears, you are still on familiar territory.

Yes m'dears, you have only crossed a bridge not swum an ocean, to get here.' The atmosphere in the classroom was different; he looked around and smiled, took a deep breath and continued.

'Now, I am going to teach you a wonderful subject, English Literature. Now, what is English Literature?' He was going to answer the question himself but the European boy at the back of the class put up his hand.

'Books from England, Sir,' the boy said.

A lopsided smile broke out on Mr. Sylvester's face. 'What is your name?'

'Peter Johnson, Sir.'

'I like that, Peter, I like that. But I have to confess I hadn't that answer in mind when I asked the question. But you are right. Thank you for reminding us. Now what else is English Literature apart from books from England?'

The African girl on June's right put up her hand and said, 'Novels, poems, plays and essays, Sir.'

'Excellent!' Mr. Sylvester declared, impressed. 'What is your name, my dear girl?'

'Paula Duncan, Sir.'

'Thank you, Paula.'

He wrote 'novels, poems, plays, essays' under 'Literature' on the blackboard, then turned and picked up one of his books. 'This is one of the greatest novelists in the world, one of his great novels, *Great Expectations* by Charles Dickens, an Englishman. You will read the novel later, in your fourth year, but we will study extracts from it in the form of comprehension lessons. In the fifth form you will study another great English author, my favourite author, George Eliot; we will read *Mill on the Floss,* but there are many delights awaiting you before that.' Some students grumbled and complained that they hated reading stories. Mr. Sylvester made a face and shook his head. 'I pity the person who does not read,' he declared. 'Through language we discipline our thoughts.' He waited for silence then continued, 'I expect you have all done school plays so you know what plays are?' Everyone nodded. 'We will study the greatest playwright in the world, William Shakespeare – the experience of your life awaits you when we study Shakespeare, my chickens.' Many students groaned, and Mr. Sylvester declared that he was extremely disappointed in them. 'Now poetry, does anyone know a good poem? Not nonsense rhymes now, but a serious poem.'

Paula Duncan put up her hand again and told Mr. Sylvester that she knew a poem by William Blake, 'Tiger Tiger'.

Mr. Sylvester looked very impressed by this and asked Paula to recite it.

June listened to Paula with admiration as she recited the poem in a clear, confident voice. No one was laughing or sniggering. When Paula finished her recitation Mr. Sylvester did not have to praise her again, he looked so proud of her. Paula sat down and exchanged a smile with June.

Mr. Sylvester said, 'There is another English novelist we will study in comprehension...' There were more groans. 'Jane Austen, who will show us the genteel side of life...'

Someone asked, 'What that mean, Sir?'

Mr. Sylvester asked, 'Who knows the meaning of "genteel"? Anyone?'

Someone said, 'Gentle sir, it must come from "gentle".'

'All right, let's start from "gentle". Someone tell me the meaning of "gentle".'

'Kind,' June volunteered. Someone else said, 'Quiet.' A boy said, 'Good.'

Mr. Sylvester spoke, 'You would normally use those words about a person, wouldn't you?' He waited for some to nod in agreement. 'But if you wanted to describe a group of people, a class of people who were like that, what word would you use?'

Peter Johnson said, 'Genteel.'

'Yes, genteel describes a way of life of a certain class of people who have certain aspirations, who aspire to genteelness, as in the novels of Jane Austen. She writes about the middle class of England...' As Mr. Sylvester described the aspirations of these people June felt that their aspirations were like Lucille's. Was that the word to describe what Lucille wanted: gentility?

Now Peter Johnson was asking, 'Does "gentile" come from "genteel", Sir.'

Mr. Sylvester puffed out his cheeks and pretended to look serious. 'Well you have asked a wonderfully interesting question there, Peter. Do you know what "gentile" means?'

'No Sir,' Peter Johnson replied.

'Anyone know?'

Merle Searwar, the girl on June's left, said, 'It comes from the bible, Sir. Gentiles and Jews.'

'Say more,' Mr. Sylvester coaxed, but she just shrugged. He shook his head disapprovingly. 'Yes it is a biblical word, "gentile", used to describe a race of people who are not Jews, the race of people who created New Testament Christianity. You will learn all about it in your Religious Education classes. I can only simplify it now. Let us say for the time being that gentiles are Christians, not Jews.'

Paula Duncan asked, 'Am I a gentile sir? I am Christian.'

Mr. Sylvester sighed and said, 'Technically you are gentile.'

A voice, a boy's, came from the back, 'Gentiles white, Sir, not black like we.'

Mr. Sylvester asked the boy his name, and the reply came back, 'Repu Tiwari, Sir. I am a Hindu; my father is a pandit and he told me gentiles are white people.'

Mr. Sylvester sighed. 'Sit down, boy.'

Whether 'gentile' was linked to the word 'genteel' – everyone lost interest, including Mr. Sylvester. It was too complicated, but the question remained in June's mind. Was Lucille a gentile and was this why she wanted gentility? Was Repu Tiwari right? Could black people like Africans and Indians be gentiles?

8. A FAILURE

It was only twelve o'clock and her first day at school was over. Mr. Sylvester had dismissed the class and gone. She could feel the saucepan at her feet. The food was cold now, and despite herself she was ashamed of the saucepan. It made everyone think of sugar plantation workers and the things about them that Sarah Beardsley scorned: cowdung, coconut oil, latrines and lice. Lucille and Cyrus always said that people who mocked the poor in this country should remember that they made it prosper through their labour; no one would be interested in British Guiana if it did not produce sugar. But Lucille had made her scrub herself with Lifebuoy soap, had dusted her heavily with Yardley's talcum powder and sprayed her uniform with perfume. Her uniform, books and bicycle were brand new. She was like a new person except for the saucepan which every canecutter and sugar estate labourer carried to work. None of the other country children were turned out as well as she, but none of them had made the mistake of bringing a saucepan of food to school.

Paula Duncan touched her arm, 'What's your name again?'

'June Lehall. I really like your poem. I live near a forest, and the farmers say that sometimes they see a tiger. Where you learn it?'

'My father has a book with drawings and poems, "Tiger" is his favourite poem.'

'I really like it.'

'You can come to my house in Winkle and read it.'

'Where Winkle?'

'Behind the school. Is only a small village.'

'A village here in New Amsterdam?'

'Yes, my father say all here used to be plantations, and Winkle is still like a village.'

'I come from a plantation, New Dam.'

'I never been on a plantation.'

'You can come and play with me. We can ride about. Plenty space in Canefields. We can go to the forest and swim in the river. I go with my father. We catch and cook fish and pick fruits.'

Paula laughed. 'I don' know if my parents will 'low me. I can't swim in a pool even. You can swim good?'

'Yes, since I was small.'

'I wish I could swim.'

They did not know what else to say to each other. They looked around them. It was harder now they were not calling names or abusing each other, but trying to make friends. June looked at the girl on her left, Merle Searwar, who returned her look calmly. She did not look unfriendly but she was not in a hurry to make friends with anyone either. All through the earlier confusion Merle Searwar had remained aloof and bored.

Merle asked, 'You are from the country?'

'Yes. New Dam.'

'My mother is from the country, from the Corentyne. She is Hindu but my father is Christian. You are Christian?'

June had been baptised and confirmed a Christian although she did not feel like one in spirit. Still, by law she was a Christian, so eventually she answered 'Yes,' but she added quickly, 'My mother is the real Christian but she is Indian. My father is not whole Indian, he is Chinese too but he was brought up as a Hindu. He don't like Christianity, and me neither.'

She expected Merle to laugh at her, she sounded so confused, but Merle looked more interested, though still was not eager for conversation. Merle Searwar was like an adult in her self-assurance.

June asked, 'You live in New Amsterdam?'

Merle smiled and the dimples showed in her cheeks, making her look prettier. Merle, Tina Jaikarran, Fazia Bacchus, and Louise Sampson – they were the prettiest girls in the class, the ones Lucille would admire and want June to be like; not just pretty, sophisticated looking too, not a tomboy like she, like Lavender and like Cynthia Simmonds, or plain like Paula and a few of the other girls. Appearance was important to Lucille.

Merle did not answer her question but asked her one instead, 'You want me to keep your books at my house to save you going home with all of them? You're not supposed to bring all your books the first day you know. My brother was in the sixth form and he told me we do nothing on the first day, only listen to teachers talking, hear speeches and get our timetable. Let me keep your books for you.'

June turned to look at Paula who was listening. Paula encouraged her. 'Yes, let Merle keep your books. I will keep some too.'

June shook her head. 'No, my mother will vex. These books expensive.'

Merle shrugged, got up and left, alone.

Paula said, 'Her family, the Searwars, are the richest in New Amsterdam.'

'That's why she's stuck-up?'

'Not like some of them...' Paula pointed to the girls in the row behind them, 'who like to show off as if they rich. I went to convent school with all of them. We all know each other from then.'

Lavender, looking angry, came to her desk. 'You not going home?' she snapped, looking Paula up and down scornfully.

June was thinking about leaving her books with Paula. She told Lavender. 'I might go with Paula to Winkle and leave my books at her house. You come too.'

Lavender snapped, 'Her house! You don' know her. Who is she?'

The girls were beginning to notice Lavender. They were staring at her and Lavender was very conscious of it. She was not well-dressed like the other girls. Her skirt was not made of wool like everyone else's, but of the cheapest cotton, with as little cloth as possible. It was thin and transparent with hardly

81

any pleats and no room for Lavender to grow into. She wore no slip so you could see through the skirt, and you could see her brassiere too, through her blouse which was made from cheap, thin cotton. She was the only girl in the class with large breasts. If Lavender had been well dressed and pretty they might have envied her for her breasts, but she was ill-dressed and untidy. Her hair was in tiny plaits, not straightened like Paula Duncan's and Louise Sampson's and tied neatly back with ribbons. She was not wearing leather shoes either but the canvass shoes which country children wore to school.

June decided to leave with Lavender. At the door she turned to see Annie still sitting at her place. She asked Lavender, 'You spoke to her?'

'Who? The white girl?'

'Yes.'

Lavender stuck her nose in the air and sucked her teeth. 'She is too damn stuck up. I talk to her and she 'in say one word to me.' June saw now why Lavender was in such a temper. The group of boys at the back of the class were giggling among themselves and pointing at her. Lavender was doing her best to ignore them by turning her back, sticking her nose in the air and looking as if she did not care. June could not think what to do or say to the boys to stop them.

She asked Lavender, 'Why you don't tell them something?'

Lavender looked angry and confused, 'Tell them something? I would more than tell then something! I would give them all a good kick.'

'Tell your father, your mother, complain to the headmaster. Or just try and ignore them; don't let them see they bothering you.' But they *were* bothering Lavender. She declared, 'I don' like this stuck-up school. I not coming back, you see all these chil'ren here? All is doctor or lawyer or overseer chil'ren. They don' want we here. Look at them. That green-eye coolie you sittin' near t'ink she is great an' that black one with her hair press an' with red ribbon look like butter won' melt in her mouth...' There were tears in Lavender's eyes which she was fighting back.

'Lavender, let's go and get your books. Don' worry with them.'

'I don' know where to go and get books.'

'We have to go to the headmaster and ask about secondhand books.' She remembered Annie. 'Wait here and I will go and see if the white girl all right.'

Lavender pulled her back. 'Don' go near her, man. She sick! She nearly vomit.'

'That is exactly what I worried about. The teachers don' know she is sick.' She went to Annie and sat beside her. 'Annie, how you getting home?'

Annie looked June up and down but said nothing.

June asked her again, 'How you getting home? When the bus coming?'

Peter Johnson joined them. 'It's all right,' he said, 'I telephoned my father. They are sending a land rover for us.'

His voice was like Overseer Beardsley's voice, an overseer's voice. She drew back from him. 'I was making sure she was all right.'

He smiled. 'What is your name?'

She did not answer, only walked away towards Lavender who was waiting for her at the door.

Lavender said, 'He is Overseer Johnson son. You know bald-head Johnson? They say he like to rape women.' Lavender nudged her. 'You better look out and don' talk to him.' Lavender giggled.

June rebuked her. 'You too stupid! No wonder those boys could provoke you!'

They walked to the bicycle shed. The school was almost empty of students. Only the stragglers remained, making their way slowly from the classrooms, riding their bicycles along the paths, towards the exits.

Lavender continued to talk about the overseers. 'You see the black girl with the press-hair and white ribbons? Her father is Overseer Sampson, a black overseer, first black overseer in the world! He black like tar and living with them white people. I don' know how they could do it. I would never live with white people. Look at her in the plantation bus, you will see her there with all them white children, and she black like tar, she and them two coolies, their father turn overseer too, overseering their own mati-coolie...' Lavender was working herself into a temper again.

The bicycle was buried under a stack of bicycles which had collapsed. June asked Lavender, 'Lavender, help me get out my bike. Hold these ones up...'

Now Lavender turned on her. 'Why I should help you? You think I is your slave?'

Now June's temper flared too. 'You won' help me? Awright! We'll see if I tow you to school again. You see if I stop and give you a lift to school again.'

While June struggled with the bicycles, Lavender watched, holding June's books. When the bike was free Lavender helped her strap the books to the carrier.

June offered. 'Come, let's go and get the books from the headmaster now...'

Lavender shook her head. 'I not going.'

'If you don't have books tomorrow you will be in a lot'a trouble. You see that Mrs. Farley. She look like she don' make fun with that cane.'

Lavender tugged at her plaits. 'I 'in frighten her.'

'Well I frighten her. You would do well to be frightened of her...'

'I don' care.'

Lavender was brewing up trouble for herself. She reminded June of the children at St. Peter's primary school in Canefields who decided to stay in permanent trouble with the bad teachers, to fight them and the school, take all the whippings they could give.

June shook her head. 'What Miss Rachael will say?' Rachael Jones was the opposite of Lavender. It was hard to believe they were sisters. Rachael was beautiful, she sang like an angel in church and had qualified as a teacher two years ago. Now she was engaged to be married to Mr. Sam.

'Look Lavender,' June snapped. 'I not begging you to go and get your own books. Last time I telling you – let us go and get the books.'

Lavender looked betrayed. Suddenly, she lifted her hand and cuffed June hard on the shoulder, so hard she lost her grip on the bicycle and it collapsed to the ground.

'Who the hell you think you are?' Lavender berated her. 'Now you playing high and mighty, great like the rest of them. You think I di'n see you talking to them white people, to that rich coolie and show-off Paula Duncan – getting up and showing off how she know poem!' She cuffed June again and again, shouting, 'I don' want come to this school. I don' want no second-hand books. All'a you got new books!' Lavender was hysterical, screaming, shouting, tears streaming down her face.

June, with blows raining down on her, was able to pick up her bicycle and use it to shield herself from Lavender, turning the bicycle, pointing it at Lavender and threatening to ride into her. Lavender turned and ran away. She disappeared behind the auditorium.

June followed her. When she reached the gate she looked for Lavender and saw her hiding under the low bottomhouse of the auditorium. She called to her. 'Lavender, come let us go home.'

Lavender shouted, 'Just because you dress like them they helping you. Well, you 'in stay like them! They is not you friend. You think you great but you 'in one bit great. You wait, one of these good days you will find out you 'in no big shot...' Feeling her body and feelings bruised, June rolled her bicycle over the narrow bridge and began to cycle homewards, towards the Dolphin swingbridge.

A strong breeze was blowing across the exposed highway and open landscape. She did not get very far on her bicycle. When she tried to ride against the breeze it stopped her with a force and energy that brought tears of frustration to her eyes.

In the end she gave up and walked the length of the highway to the swingbridge. More experienced, stronger cyclists braved the breeze, pitting themselves against it, overtaking her and moving in almost slow motion. Cyclists going in the opposite direction, towards the school, came racing towards her, the momentum of the downward slope bearing them along a good two hundred yards. There were a few draycarts along the road, small draycarts pulled by donkeys, slow on wooden wheels; larger ones on three pairs of car tyres, pulled by a horse or pony. The traffic of buses and taxis was slower at this time of day, increasing later, as the workers began to return home to the villages. There were no other students on the road. Many had gone into New Amsterdam to explore the town, and a large group of children had collected under the tall jacaranda tree outside the school to wait for the Corentyne buses. She thought about Lavender huddled like a dog under the bottom-house, and saw herself small and weak against the strong breeze, dwarfed by the landscape and distance around her, struggling towards home, and felt that somewhere in this first day at the new school there had been a failure, something had gone wrong that would never be right again.

9 DISCUSSIONS

The Dolphin swingbridge was deserted. She stopped to rest on the platform, leaning her bicycle against the rail and leaning over to look down at the Canje waters. The river was so polluted and cloudy here it seemed to sweat in the heat. It was at ease though because the fishing on the banks had ceased, except for a lone fisherman who was casting his net downriver. Further downriver a large foreign ship was waiting for the water to rise before making the journey upstream. Perhaps it was a bauxite ship, it was so discoloured, white paint smeared with rust-red patches. The writing on the ship was foreign. Perhaps it was a Russian ship. They said that Cheddi Jagan was going to turn this country into a Russian country. If that was true why did they bother to go to school and learn English history, religion, language and literature. It was all going to be useless to them when the country changed. They might as well learn Russian language, geography and so on. What was it all for if it was going to be useless to her, useless to the country? One day she would have to learn all over again, unlearn everything she was learning now. Suddenly these thoughts made her laugh out loud. It did her good to feel it was all absurd and useless. To think that all this fuss could be for nothing – Lucille's fuss and Lavender's fuss – it was a joke. The laughter relaxed her.

She stayed on the bridge for a long time, enjoying the sounds of the water, the play of the light on the surface, waiting for the appearance of a fish and its quick movement as it almost leapt out of the water to dive away again. The coconut trees swayed and danced in the breeze far away in the grove. She could see the tiny figures of people there, men and boys, as they moved from tree to tree with sugar sacks on their backs.

The group on the ground waited patiently while the climbers scaled up the trees, moving upwards with rhythmic climbing movements, eyes pointed upwards, watchful for falling coconuts, stopping once in a while to adjust the straps on their feet or rest. There was so much space on the land, plenty for the eye to take in, people busy on the land, waterways to travel, ground to clear and plant and build on. You looked around you and it was all going on – space and living, but it was such a miserable country, poor people living like prisoners in crowded villages where they could not plant or settle as they pleased, could not speak as equals, as men, women, human beings, to the overseers. They said that many of the overseers were British men who had fought in the second world war in Germany and the Far East and had been prisoners of war in those places, that they still behaved as if they were in prison camps, only this time they were the ruling army and the sugar workers were the prisoners, that there was some kind of revenge or sickness in the way they overseered the plantations. If you did not live in a plantation village you did not have to put up with that, but your freedom was limited too, you did not get far before you came up against one kind of restriction or another. Look at Cheddi Jagan – the British Governor here and the British Government in England put him in jail as soon as he tried to be leader of this country. Was Guiana really just a big prison camp run by the British? If it was, all the freedom of the land that your eyes saw was just an illusion, a dream.

All the journey home, the villages lay sweating in the heat. Though her hat covered and shielded her head and face from the sun, only at the borders between the villages where the land was open and expansive did the breeze cool her. Lucille would be waiting at home to hear about her first day.

The cottage was cool in the shade, with the guinep tree on one side and the baskets of fern clothing its lower walls, and the vegetable garden cooling the ground everywhere with shade. Cyrus had fitted extra sheets of zinc to extend from the roof and keep the walls of the cottage shaded too. Lucille was sitting at the open window, working at the sewing machine when June arrived home. Lucille looked happy. Today was a success for her because her dream for June had come true, because she had managed to provide everything needed for June to go to the best school in Berbice. She felt proud and happy, feelings which living on a plantation did not bring every day. From now on June would be a different child, they would be a different family, free people.

Indoors, after June had changed, cooled herself with a glass of iced water, eaten her lunch, and answered all of Lucille's questions, the memory of Lavender under the bottom-house still bothered her. She had said nothing about Lavender and Lucille had not asked.

'You didn't ask about Lavender,' June accused Lucille.

Lucille looked up from her sewing, surprised by the accusation in her daughter's voice. 'What about Lavender?'

'Lavender has no books. We have to get her some books, and her uniform look terrible. Tell her mother to buy a good uniform for her. She had on yatching shoes, old ones. Nobody comb her hair properly. All her bubby showing through her blouse...'

Lucille shouted at June, 'Be quiet! Don't you shout at me! And don't say 'bubby', say 'breast'. Use English!'

'The boys, they were tormenting Lavender. Everybody look at her like dirt.'

'Which boys?'

'I don' know them. They come from the Corentyne, or West Coast.'

'You keep away from those boys. That school used to be an exclusive school; now all kinds go there.'

'When you will go and see Miss Jones and help out with Lavender?'

'I can't help out.'

'Why?'

'Tell me how I can help out. Eh? tell me?'

'Sew her uniform.'

'With what? You think money grow on trees? Your father is up in arms about school fees and the money we had to spend

89

getting your books and uniform. You want me to do the same for every child in this village. Who do you think I am? The Governor?'

'Well talk to Miss Jones and advise her. Tell her to buy better cloth.'

'With what? Mr. Jones is only a guttersmith. Mrs. Jones, Harriet, is a servant with Overseer Mendonca.'

'Rachael can help out.'

'Rachael is engaged to be married. She gave her two year's salary to her parents, now she wants to live her own life. She will still give them a little bit but she and Mr. Sam are going to rent land and a cottage from the overseers – a big expense. How much do you think teachers earn? They earn very little.'

There was a long silence between them. June was leaning against the partition which separated the bedroom from the kitchen. Lucille, still sitting at her sewing machine, gave June a long and bitterly disappointed look. June was spoiling all the satisfaction of today. She returned to her sewing, saying, 'Lavender will just have to learn to look after herself and do the best she can.'

'She hit me.'

Lucille turned around. 'Who hit you?'

'Lavender.'

'She hit you?'

'Yes.'

Lucille drew in a deep breath. 'Good Lord.' She sighed, and thought for a long time, then asked, 'Did the teachers or anyone else see her do it?'

'No.'

'Well, just keep away from her too. You did anything to provoke her?'

'No. I was trying to get her to go and get her second-hand books from the headmaster so she can keep up with lessons tomorrow. But she didn't want second-hand books because everybody else has new books, new everything.'

'How you know? She said so?'

'No, but I know.'

'You know too much for your own good. You always know

90

what everybody thinking although they don't say so,' Lucille accused. 'You should mind your own business and leave other people to mind theirs.'

'You said neighbours should help each other, especially in times of trouble.'

'Yes but this is different. You and Lavender are schoolgirls. Lavender just has to try and pull herself together. There is nothing wrong with her, not like Annie Beardsley. I know that is what you are thinking. And if she is going to start fighting at school that is her lookout. You are to keep far away from her. Do you hear me?'

'Tell Nurse.'

'Tell her what?'

'That Lavender fighting at school.'

'You know that is one thing Nurse doesn't tolerate, girls fighting. I think it is best if we leave it a few weeks. Tomorrow, Lavender might be all right for all you know. Now, stop all this nonsense. Tell me about Mrs. Farley. You haven't said anything about Mrs. Farley.'

'I don't like her.'

'She's strict. But I hear she keeps the discipline in the school. Do your work and you won't cross her path.'

'She hit me.'

'Hit you? Why?'

She explained and Lucille laughed with relief. 'That is not hitting,' Lucille said. 'You love to exaggerate. You must try and get things in perspective. Now listen, Mrs. Farley has been at the school from the time it opened. She was a pupil there. That school is Mrs. Farley and Mrs. Farley is that school. Her bark is worse than her bite. You are not to blow her up out of all proportions in your mind.'

'Well I don't like her. I hate her. If she ever hits me I will not take it.'

Lucille stared at June, shocked, then she calmed herself, sighed and spoke gently. 'You are a very difficult child you know, very intolerant. You are determined to see the world in your own light.'

'Don't criticise me. Mrs. Farley is the one you should

91

criticise. She shouldn't talk like that to us, without knowing us, without giving us a chance. No need for her to talk like a pig to children. That is the kind of school you want to send me to, a pig school!'

Lucille shook her finger at her, 'You! You go for the first time in your life to be among civilised people and the one you fall in with is the one with the bad influence! Bad influence is what you prefer, always, always! You don't know what is good for you! Go to your bed and stay there!'

Later that afternoon, Lucille told June to bathe and put on a good dress; they were going to the senior staff compound to visit the Sampson family. When June asked why, Lucille explained, 'I am going to ask Mrs. Sampson to see if you can travel to school on the plantation bus. I think you are finding the cycling too difficult. You came home worn out and beside yourself.'

'But we can't use the plantation bus, only white people use it.'

'Of course not. Louise Sampson uses it, and Overseer Ali's children. There are local overseers now.'

'Lavender said Louise doesn't belong with white people.'

'That Lavender is an ignorant girl, a bad apple in a good family. She has an inferiority complex and I can see you are anxious to have one too. She has no understanding how to get along with people.'

'No, Lavender is right. People should stay where they belong, with their own kind, especially when other people don' want us around them.'

The silence between them was so tense, June began to feel the start of a headache.

'What that is supposed to mean?' Lucille asked tersely.

June said nothing, not wanting to destroy Lucille's dreams, not wanting to tell her how the town girls had abused her racially, had laughed at her saucepan and treated her like nothing. She would not believe it, she might even say it was her own fault, that perhaps she had done something to provoke it.

'Are you going to answer me?' Lucille demanded.

June still said nothing.

'You know, a lot of people strike their children when nothing else will teach them sense. I don't strike you, June, not willingly, only rarely when you really try me, which you are fond of doing. I told myself the thing I want you to learn most of all is self-respect, that is why I don't like to strike you.' She paused. 'I am beginning to think I must give up trying with you, that I have failed, that you don't like what I am trying to do for you.' She clutched herself – the baby was kicking. She sat down at the kitchen table. 'I can't keep running to Nurse for help with you, we have to ask Mrs. Sampson this favour. Go on, go and get bathed and dressed. I will send for Mitch to come and take us.'

While she bathed, June steeled herself for the visit with bitter thoughts. Lucille did not know what she was doing or saying any more. What did she mean by saying that she never whipped her out of wanting her to learn self-respect? Lucille had never said anything like this to her before. Since when was self- respect the reason? She used to say it was cruel to whip children and that was why she did not do it. It used to be to do with Lucille's own principle, not a favour to her. And since when did she 'run' too often to Nurse? Nurse passed through the village every single day on her bicycle just so that people could stop her and ask for help. They put out a white flag if they wanted her urgently, but she always called out to Lucille from the public road and liked to stop here for a rest and cup of iced water. Since when was Nurse no use? Nothing in New Dam was good enough for Lucille any more – not even her own family, her own daughter. This education had nothing to do with her and everything to do with Lucille. That was the problem. Lucille was pretending she cared about her education when all she wanted was to get her out of New Dam into town.

Mitch came to collect them at five o' clock in his old black Prefect. In exchange for attention to his car from Cyrus, Mitch drove Lucille wherever she wanted to go. He had never had to drive her to the overseers' quarters before. He asked, 'Cyrus know you going to overseer quarters?'

'Yes thank you Mitch,' Lucille said stiffly.

At the gate, the security guard stopped them. A British soldier sat in the security hut. Mitch and Lucille were startled to see him. They had only heard about the presence of British troops; this was their first sighting of one. The security guard had to confer with the soldier before he could let them in.

Lucille asked, 'Mitch, you see the soldier?'

Mitch was beside himself with excitement. 'Jesus Lord, soldier in Canefields! Wait till Boysie hear!'

'I wonder why they bring them here.'

'Must be to station them with they mati white people. They can only stay on plantation. This place set up like army barracks anyway, with everybody in compound. Well yes, first time British soldier come to Canefields!' Mitch became irritated at being kept waiting. He fretted. 'Everywhere you want go in this place you got to ask permission. Just to shif y'u backside you have to wait till they say is awright.' He put his head through the window and yelled. 'Hey man! How long we must roast in this sun?'

Lucille cautioned him. 'Look, Mitch, mind your language and manners.'

The soldier and security guard came to the car. It was the soldier who put his face to the window and spoke. 'I believe this is just a social call?' He was young and not suntanned like the overseers. It was obvious he had only just come from England.

Mitch could not make out a word he said, and turned to Lucille and asked, 'Wha' he say?'

Lucille spoke to the soldier as if she was not sure he understood her language. 'The Sampsons. It is the Sampsons.'

Lucille was flustered by the soldier who looked just as anxious to understand her. 'You know the Sampsons?'

The soldier did not fully understand even what Lucille was saying. They were baffled by each other's accents. He turned to the security guard and asked him to translate what Lucille was saying.

'They going to visit Overseer Sampson, Sir,' the guard explained. 'I telephone Mistress Sampson. She say she is

94

expecting them. It is all right to send them up.'

The soldier did not understand a word the security guard said either, but he shrugged and waved them in.

Mitch sucked his teeth. He was not curious about the soldier any more. 'How they could send people who can't understand a word we say to patrol we with gun. Look Lucille, you see he rifle? He would shoot we down dead no question asked. You sure you want go in this compound? If Cyrus vex with me, wha' I mus' tell he?'

'You tell him I ask you to bring me here.'

Mitch sighed and drove into the compound. These houses, unlike the cottages in the junior staff compound, were set further in from the public road. Mitch had said that the plantation was set out like army barracks. June saw it for the first time. Mitch was right. Only Overseer Beardsley let plenty of trees and shrubs grow in his garden and make hiding places. No other house in the compound was so concealed. The wide open spaces of lawns exposed everything and although there were many tall jacaranda trees they were well spaced out at intervals which allowed a clear view across the compound from all directions. These houses were not as large as the Beardsley's but they were still imposing, tall and elegant on stout concrete pillars, their white coat of paint fresh against the green lawns. They passed a house with a vegetable garden. A man stood in the grove of papaya trees and watered the leaves profusely, letting the jet of water rise in the air and fall in a shower to wash the leaves until they sagged.

'What a waste of water,' Lucille commented enviously.

They passed servants out walking the children, and labourers weeding the flower beds. The milk boy was delivering milk at one house, parking his goods cycle in the drive, then making his way up the back stairs with the large milk pail on his back, pint ladle in his hand. Milk, groceries and newspapers were delivered to the overseers' back doors. The people in the villages used tinned and powdered milk. If you wanted fresh milk you had to have your own cow or goat, or get permission from the overseers to buy milk from their dairy. Some of the women in New Dam clubbed together to pay small boys to

95

walk the mile to the dairy and fetch them fresh milk once a week; it had to be done early in the morning or late in the afternoon when it was cool and the sun would not turn the milk. Only farmers near the forest owned cows or goats and when they had excess milk they would cycle through the villages with their milk pails and ladles.

Mitch stopped to ask a weeder for directions to the Sampson's house. She pointed to the last row of houses, to the last house in that row. The canefield grew very close to this row of houses, and there was a playground on the stretch of lawn between the canefield and the house. Children played there and June saw Louise Sampson, Fazia Bacchus, Peter Johnson and a boy who looked like Fazia's brother, among them, but they were mostly European children. A servant was taking clothes off the clothes line under the bottomhouse. The breeze was blowing in strongly over the canefields, filling the air with the scent of young cane, billowing out the clothes on the line. On the lawn which separated the Sampson's house from the next house in the row, several white sheets were bleaching, held down by large, bleached stones at their corners. It was a sign of how clean and dry the ground was here, that white sheets could be put out to dry on the grass. They would have been laid out since mid-morning when the sun sharpened, and left to absorb the heat and light through noon and early afternoon. Now, the sun was weaker and the breeze was cooling everything. The sheets were cooling, blue-white from their day's bleaching.

Mitch promised to return for them at six thirty, then drove back to the gates, towards New Dam. Louise Sampson came running to meet them.

'Hello June, you are in my class, Form Two,' Louise greeted her.

June did not respond, and sensed Lucille's irritation. They followed Louise up the front stairs. June remembered how she had to use the back stairs at the Beardsleys. It was a well known fact in New Dam that the overseers and junior staff did not permit people from the villages to use their front stairs. If you had any business at their houses, like the milk boy, carpenters and electricians, you presented yourself at the back door. But Lucille and Mrs. Sampson were members of the Mothers Union at the church and that made them equals. Their Christian god made them equals, but their husbands were not equals. If Lucille were in a better mood June might have had the courage to tell her so, to tell her that Mrs. Sampson would not have the power to get permission for her to travel on the plantation bus. There was one set of rules for church, one set for the overseers and another for New Dam. The church had no power over the overseers; it was the opposite that was true. The estate gave land to the church and to St. Peter's primary school which was run by the church. The overseers maintained the church. The priests were not treated with any respect at all by the overseers. People said that relations were always bad between the priests and the overseers because the priests criticised the plantation for the living conditions in the villages. When they criticised too much they were made to suffer. Every four years, a new priest was sent out from England.

Mrs. Sampson came to the door to meet them. 'Hello, Lucille my dear. How are you?'

'Well, thank you, Anna. And you?'

They went on exchanging pleasantries like this for a few more minutes, in the way people did at church. Christianity and June's education mattered more than anything else to Lucille and June tried her best to let them matter least to her. She did not take that attitude to spite Lucille but because she did not think it made Lucille happy to try so hard to be what she was not; June felt she took her attitude for the best; at least she hoped it was for the best, that it was somehow the best thing for herself and for Lucille. Standing with the two women as they indulged in the same conversation they had every Sunday after mass she still felt a familiar affection for them, but affection mixed with sadness.

'I never see you at church, June, Mrs. Sampson remarked.

Lucille sighed. 'Well, you know June. Wild horses wouldn't drag her to the church door.'

'Come and sit down.' Mrs. Sampson waved towards the

Morris chairs. 'Would you like to sit indoors or on the verandah? I myself don't like sitting in the broad daylight in full public view on the verandah.'

'Let us sit in here then,' Lucille said.

Louise stood by herself, near the door, obedient, waiting for her mother to speak to her.

Mrs. Sampson turned to Louise. 'Louise, go and tell the servant to bring some lime drink. Tell her to put it on a tray, and to use coasters.'

Louise went to the kitchen and they sat down, Lucille and Mrs. Sampson sitting opposite each other. Mrs. Sampson complained about her servants. She found them very difficult. She put so much effort into training them, then they always left her for the white overseers. Lucille said nothing, only listened. It was not a subject she could hold a conversation about but she listened with real interest and sympathy. June listened, hearing the difference between this friendship of Lucille's and her friendships with women in the village, not able to decide which was closer. Lucille and Mrs. Sampson understood each other's aspirations and because of this they were close, but it was not the closeness which existed between women friends in the village, the closeness of people with the same struggles, trials and tribulations who did not just talk about them and listen sympathetically but did things together all the time – helping each other give birth, mind the old, bury the dead, care for the sick and contain the criminal elements.

In the village Lucille had involved herself in everything, though not this last year, with the pregnancy and June starting school in New Amsterdam. Already, there was another Lucille who was vanishing into June's memory, the woman who was closer to Cyrus, who cooked dhal, roti and curry in the kitchens of the other women, taking turns every Sunday to cook for the men when they formed weeding gangs to clear the bushes, clean the drains, mend each other's cottages and build up failing dams to keep out the floods when it rained heavily or the tide of the Canje overflowed. That was a younger, happier Lucille. Now she was getting older. They said women aged rapidly here. Perhaps Lucille was feeling it was time to give up the struggle, that she wanted an easier life as she got older, she wanted something better instead of this struggle for an existence that did not improve their prospects for the future, did not bring a better life for the children. Boysie said it was better to fight against the overseers and force them to improve their lives, to rebuild the hospital they had just pulled down, give them running water and electricity and better pay to educate their children in the way they wanted to. Lucille did not like Boysie's attitude. She saw fighting the overseers as increasing their difficulties, she did not believe like Boysie that they could win a better life through confrontation. Cyrus believed that they did not need the overseers, but needed only to learn to use their own resources to build their own community, and to pass on this tradition to the children. Beneath their everyday lives this struggle of ideas went on constantly. Now here was Lucille putting her ideas into practice at Mrs. Sampson's house, come here to see if the local overseer's wife would share her own new privileges with them.

When Louise returned with the servant who was carrying a tray of drinks, she remained apart, standing near the door. While they drank their lime drink, Mrs. Sampson continued to talk about the difficulties of being a local woman in the overseer's quarters. Her servants did not respect her and she did not mix socially with the other overseers. Their friends were from New Amsterdam. She liked to visit them and go to the cinema, to weddings, funerals, christenings and Christmas and new year parties there, but she was not really a part of the social circle there and they did not get many invitations.

When June finished her drink, Mrs. Sampson told Louise to take her out to play.

As soon as they were outdoors, Louise became different, skipping and dancing down the stairs, her blue ribbons fluttering in her hair.

Louise laughed and pointed to the playground. 'Come and play.' June followed her as she led the way, but halfway across the lawn she became apprehensive about playing with the senior compound children and told Louise she would wait under the house until their mothers finished their conversation.

99

Louise liked to laugh, she laughed whenever she spoke, except when she was in her mother's company. 'Come and play nuh?' she coaxed.

June sat on the long trestle table under the house. Louise did not go to play with her friends, but stayed with June under the bottomhouse and ran round and round touching each pillar as she went. The flooring was so high under these houses you could hold big weddings and wakes here. The bottomhouses in New Dam were a quarter of the size of this one. The old logies in Old Dam hardly had a bottomhouse; they were only high enough for the chicks, chickens, cats and dogs to roam under. People in the overseers' houses had nothing to fear from floods, rodents and crawling creatures from the mud, bush and canefields. The concrete pillars here were very tall and exposed to the driving rain, hot sun and strong breeze which would blow or wash or dry such creatures away before they could reach the tophouse. Even if they did reach the tophouse, the fine mesh screens would keep them out. The overseers were safe in their houses here. Even British soldiers came from England to protect them.

Round and round Louise ran, waving her arms like a butterfly, her blue organdie dress and hair ribbons like kite-tails in the breeze. She was trying to attract June's attention. June did not feel like playing. Ever since she left St. Peter's school and was not allowed to play in the villages any more, she was forgetting what it was like to play.

Louise came to sit at the table and began to ask all kinds of questions. What kind of books did she read, what kind of clothes did she have, who were her friends in New Dam, how did she spend her time in New Dam, what was it like to cycle to school, did she get money from her parents and how much, did they have a radio and did she listen to the BBC World Service, and learn to play the piano and violin and listen to classical music? Louise was so friendly June found herself talking very freely to her. No they did not have a radio, only Mr. Easen had a big Ferguson and it hardly worked but he had a record player and one New Year's eve Cyrus and Lucille had gone there and danced the 'bop' to

Glenn Miller records. June wanted to tell Louise about her old friends from St. Peter's but she was afraid that she would laugh at them. She decided to say nothing about them until she was sure Louise was not a mocker. Just the Indian names might make her laugh. But June told her about how different the kind of dancing done at the Hindu barriat was, how the bridegroom's friends came to the bride's village in bus loads with the jukebox blaring Indian songs and calypsos and how they danced, winding-up their hips and making signs and gestures to court the girls who lined up on the stairs and at the windows to watch them. She described the public dances at the school hall where the music was different: Nat Cole and Platters songs, Sparrow calypsos and pop songs – that was where you could hear all the latest music coming into the country, and the dancing in there was just as wild, but then the dancing at queh queh, kali-mai and steelband tramps could get really out of hand.

'Louise asked suspiciously, 'How come you know all that? Your mother allow you to go?'

'She stop me now, but long ago when we used to live in Old Dam everything used to happen in front your eyes. Now everybody has their own yard.'

'What about obeah? You ever see any obeah?'

'Mother took Father to the kali-mai when he was really ill once. Then she had to call in Miss K from Pheasant to work good obeah on the house and then she went to the Chinese obeah lady in New Amsterdam.'

'My mother say obeah is the devil's work, that they should put people in jail for it.'

'People use it for good things too, but I hear sometimes about revenge spells.'

Louise was taking all this very seriously, not laughing at all. To her, it was something to fear, black magic, yet she was curious to know if it really was evil. 'I would like to come and visit your house.' She wanted to find out things for herself; June liked that.

'You not frighten of the soldier at the gate?' June asked.

Louise laughed. 'Why I should frighten? I heard that they were coming here long before they come. They broadcast it on the BBC World Service. They come from Scotland, they call them the Argyll regiment. Then you have the East Anglians, the Coldstreams...'

'New Dam people frighten. Mitch gone to tell them that the soldiers come.'

Louise sighed wearily. 'You shouldn't frighten. If you not a communist you shouldn't frighten. They only come to control the communists.'

'We don't have communists in New Dam.'

'Cheddi Jagan is a communist. They said so on the BBC.'

'Cheddi Jagan don't live in New Dam.'

'No, but he lives in Port Mourant on the Corentyne. He goes there every weekend to see his family.'

'Not everybody in New Dam support him. You can't believe everything you hear. You don't know anything about us. You shouldn't judge people without knowing them. I don't know a single communist. Boysie don't support Jagan one hundred per cent. He says Jagan has no experience of politics at all, that he and Burnham just come from school abroad and want to run the country.'

Louise laughed loudly and ran away to run round and round the pillars again, her arms spread wide as she ran.

Louise was a funny girl – one minute she made June feel like a small girl again but the next minute she said wrong-headed things which made June feel like giving her a good long lecture about this world, then Louise laughed at her when she lectured her. If they were going to be friends it was going to be that kind of friendship, with differences between them. Louise had no malice in her so it was possible for them to be different and friends.

When Lucille and Mistress Sampson descended the stairs there was stiffness between them, especially in Lucille.

Mistress Sampson said, 'I would take you home myself but the car is at the workshop, being serviced.'

'No, it's all right,' Lucille said. 'Mitch will come soon.'

The two women stood near the flower beds in silence, Lucille too distracted to take a good look at the flowers while she had the chance. June jumped off the table, ran to Lucille and hugged her round the waist. She guessed that Mistress

Sampson must have told Lucille she was not allowed to use the plantation bus. June was glad to see Mitch's car driving too fast through the compound, coming to take them home.

'Well goodbye, Lucille,' Mistress Sampson said.

'Goodbye Anna.

On the way home, Mitch asked Lucille if her visit to the overseer was successful and Lucille did not answer him.

June pressed Lucille to answer. 'What happen?'

Lucille was so depressed, she confided, 'I don't think Anna has it in her power to make arrangements for you to travel on the bus.'

Mitch sucked his teeth. 'Local black overseer pass fo' grass, jus' like we, when push come to shove. They have no power at all.'

Lucille went stiff. She thought Mitch was laughing at her but he was only speaking the truth.

At home, Lucille was so exhausted from the visit she went straight to bed. June busied herself, glad to be feeling useful, glad to be doing the adult jobs while Lucille slept and Cyrus was out. She felt free for the first time in a long time. She felt too that after the visit, Lucille might be a little more realistic. She lit the Tilley lamp. First, she released the pressure from the chamber, then checked the level of the fuel, then changed the wick carefully. She pumped new air into the chamber, lit the wick, feeding it carefully with the mixture of air and fuel. She was proud of this skill which Cyrus had taught her. The wrong mixture of air and fuel could blow out the wick and she would have to start all over again, using a new wick. Wicks were expensive and had to be used sparingly. There were other things he had taught her to do – soldering, sharpening cutlasses and hoes for the neighbours, and repairing and servicing the Chinese clock which used to belong to his father. He was always making up toys from bits and pieces in his workshop at Palmyra. Up to the last year she had been foot to foot behind him when he worked in the Sunday community gangs. She liked to hang around the carpentry gangs when they repaired or built houses. They used to let her hammer in nails, sand floors and fetch and carry tools and materials. She used to

103

follow the jeweller and tinsmith when they came to New Dam with their wares. She liked to watch the jeweller with his eyeglass stuck in his eye, all his fine tools spread out on a black cloth on the ground as he repaired elaborate necklaces and earrings. He only opened his glass and wood case when he was sure someone wanted to buy his handiwork. The wrist and ankle bangles, made of heavy Guianese gold in Indian designs, were most popular with people. People would save up for years for one of his bangles. He used to let her touch the tiny scales and weights which he used. He and the tinsmith liked to stay in a village the whole day, taking their time, reporting news and gossip from villages as far away as Skeldon and Mahaica, attracting audiences at each stop.

When Cyrus arrived he brought home the smell of grease and petrol with him as usual. Two buckets of clean water were always waiting for him in the water closet and he would collect his clean clothes from the bedroom and go straight there with the small kerosene lamp for light. Tonight he paused to tell her there was going to be a meeting at the house that night, between he, Boysie and Mr. Easen, to discuss the village council. He asked her to lay the table with snap-glasses, rum, drinks, ice and to prepare the usual snack – buttered bread and sardines seasoned with onions and ball-of-fire pepper. The smell of the food mingled with the scent of coal tar soap carried by the breeze, as Cyrus bathed, scrubbing himself vigorously with the nenwah husk and dipping calabashfuls of water to drench himself. When he was in a thoughtful mood he hummed an Indian film song during his bath and if the song really moved him he would break into full song, singing whole sentences, forgetting that Lucille did not like it.

This was the fourth village council meeting. The first three had ended in bad arguments and Lucille had asked them not to hold meetings again. Cyrus had argued that they were only preliminary meetings, and such meetings were bound to be difficult. Mr. Easen arrived when June was settled in her cot near the front door. He raised his hat at the door then kept it on. He was carrying his old case of newspaper clippings which he liked to read to everyone. He and Cyrus talked awhile until Boysie arrived.

They began to discuss the elections to come next year. They shared the same worries about the elections and the effect it was having in Canefields, but when it came to ideas about the village council Boysie and Mr. Easen began to quarrel, with Cyrus trying to reason between them. All their anxieties made them drink heavily. They had lived on the plantation all their lives and had their own strategies for dealing with the overseers and living conditions in the villages. It gave them some influence; they could organise the community when it was necessary. Now, it seemed that they were going to lose what control they did have over their lives. Now it felt as if they were small men who were being squeezed out between powerful forces which were gathering strength all the time and sweeping villages all over the country into a fight that was faceless, that had no sense. Boysie said that Jagan and Burnham were not saying anything to the people that they did not already know about their situation, that they were oppressed and so on. He said that they were behaving as if they had only just found that out and wanted to change the whole system overnight – they were too big for their boots and those people in New Dam who wanted to follow them would get too big for theirs and the overseers would starve the fight out of them, but other people would suffer with them. Everything they had won little by little would be lost by the Jagans and Burnhams, schoolboys of this world, Boysie called them, who showed no appreciation of the part played by men like them and sent their young lieutenants into the villages to appoint party representatives who had done nothing at all for the community in their whole lives and only wanted power and influence for their own vanity.

Listening to Boysie, June heard the feeling in his voice of a man who was losing everything and was desperate. At the height of his drunkenness he began to boast that this was going to be the last English plantation because of him, he would end it, not Jagan or Burnham; it would be something people in New Dam themselves would do. He ignored Mr. Easen when he reminded him that only a quarter of the overseers were English, the rest were local and besides, some were Scottish. Boysie drank more until drink removed him from the present and he began to boast about the slave rebellions of Berbice when the Dutch coffee, cotton and sugar plantations were destroyed. He had learnt the names of those plantations and began to roll them off his tongue in his Hindi accent: Jacoba, Zorg En Hoop, Volkert's Lust and so on. He had learnt the Arawak names of the creeks where he said the blood of all the races flowed: Manaribisi, Banimi, Yawara, Bisaro, Cariri, Yakasaura, Baracara. When he was helplessly drunk he began to call the Canje river by its Dutch name: Koeliroeme, and by its Arawak name: Kanya. June fell asleep with the names sounding in her ear, and Boysie saying that Indian men had learnt to live in the forest here and that was where they would go if push came to shove; they were not just plantation coolies like everybody in Guiana liked to believe, and neither were they going to be the slaves of a couple of rich Indian families who treated plantation Indians as bad as everybody; he for one had had to fight the overseers too long for that.

[handwritten margin note: plantation rebellions]

10 A WHIPPING AND A STONING

In the morning Cyrus was gone to work and Lucille was quiet and calm as she made tea, toasted the fat slices of bread round the milk pot and scrambled eggs. June could see from the way Lucille moved and the look on her face that she was afraid she would not want to go to school. They did not speak, but June filled her bucket at the well, bathed, dressed for school and sat down to eat her breakfast. Lucille said nothing to her, but put a dollar bill on the table for her lunch, collected her books and took them down to the bicycle.

At Old Dam high bridge, there was the same scene as yesterday, the crowds of workers and the overseers and foremen allocating piecework. Beyond the bridge, in the bachelor's compound, there were three lorries covered with green tarpaulin and all around the lawn there, British soldiers lay in the grass sunbathing. They were causing a lot of excitement among the young labourers who were encouraging the soldiers to come and talk to them. At the far corner of the fence where the compound ended and a small trench separated it from Manager Smith's compound, three British soldiers stood in conversation with a group of women and small boys. One of the small boys was wearing a soldier's hat, and the women were giggling in the way that women giggled when they were courting in public. They were the women who worked as servants for the overseers, and women weeders. One of the soldiers was hugging one of the women over the fence. All the soldiers were half-naked, wearing only their short trousers. Further on, at the senior staff compound, more women grouped around the two British soldiers who were on duty at the gate. It was hard to believe that these were the men who had come to shoot the communists, the men who had jailed their leaders.

The plantation bus reached the gate and Louise leaned from the window, waved and called out her name. One of the soldiers boarded the bus and it turned right into the public road. The bus overtook her and Louise waved from the rear window.

There were no soldiers at Canefield, Lucius, Cumberland or Sheet Anchor, but there was a truckful of them at the Dolphin swingbridge. They were stopping people, asking them questions then waving them on. Small boys hung round the soldiers, trying to touch their rifles and ammunition belts. June saw one of the soldiers give the boys chocolate. On the platform of the bridge a group of young men sat on the wall with a soldier; they laughed and talked together as if they knew each other well. The boys were admiring the soldier's gun and the packet of cigarettes in his hand. He looked amused and let them stroke the rifle and sniff at the cigarettes.

She was so preoccupied with worries about the meaning of the soldiers here in Berbice she had no time to worry about school, not until after she had locked her bicycle and made her way to the classroom. There at the bottom of the stairs were Rita Bachan, Lily Kissoon and Beverly Khan in a close group of their own – Rita sneered at her. She looked around for Lavender who was not there. Paula Duncan was standing with Merle Searwar; she was not sure she should join them. Louise was standing in a large group with the estate children; Louise waved and signalled for her to join them. The girls from the front row, the country girls, were sitting together on the stairs, talking among themselves and not taking notice of anyone. The boys were playing cricket on the lawn – they had something to unite them. She stood by herself, watching the compound fill up with more children. She looked at the older students, consoling herself with the thought that one day she would be older like them, a sixth former, and would leave school and be able to look after herself. Eventually, Merle and Paula came to her, but soon after that, the bell rang from the auditorium, the teachers appeared there, and began to cross the lawns for their classrooms. It was Mrs. Farley who came towards them.

Her mind was so full of the drama of the soldiers' presence in Canefields, the sight of Mrs. Farley did not frighten her at all. Yesterday in the auditorium Mr. Singh had said nothing about the British soldiers coming to Guiana, as if it was nothing, nothing at all. What did this school have to teach them? To be upright citizens who did not know that British soldiers were here with guns in their own country to terrorise poor people on the sugar estates? To be upright citizens who themselves despised poor people? As Mrs. Farley came closer she seemed not to see anyone, no faces; she had the kind of eyes which looked without seeing, like Mr. Singh, eyes which hated and despised what they saw and seemed to look away from you while still looking at you. She walked straight through the crowd of children and did not respond to the 'Good morning Miss' of some of the children. She climbed to the middle of the stairs then turned just as the bell rang a second time and waited for the children to form a line.

No one wanted to be the first group to form a queue. The estate children stood in one group, Annie Beardsley among them. The country girls formed their own group, the country boys another; Merle Searwar and Pauline Duncan stood as a pair by themselves; Merle was too rich and Pauline too bright to belong to any group. There were other pairings and three-somes it was too early to understand. They kept Mrs. Farley waiting, though gradually the queues formed, boys on one side, girls on the other, but they continued to laugh and talk in the queue, paying no attention at all to Mrs. Farley whose expression was stony.

All around the compound the lawns and paths were clear of children. The doors of other classrooms were shut and lessons were starting. Mrs. Farley was not going to say or do anything until Form Two decided to show her some respect. She was not going to ask for it. She was going to keep them outside. While she stood stonily on the stairs, they whispered and shifted in the queues. Rita and Lily were whispering about Mrs. Farley, someone sucked their teeth in irritation, others sighed wearily, and a boy at the back of the queue had the gumption to tell Mrs. Farley the sun was getting hot. Peter

Johnson made a joke about needing a tan and got some laughs. The minutes ticked by until their restlessness and patience wore into anxiety. Mrs. Farley's face was even harder now. She came down the stairs slowly and walked between the two queues, to the end, then returned to the front of the queue. There was a giggle from the middle of the boy's queue and she swung around, strode to the boy who had giggled, took hold of him by the ear and pulled him to the front of the queue. It was Rabindranauth Jekir, who was from New Amsterdam, and who was dressed poorly in cheap cottons, like Lavender. His hair was slicked down and he smelt of coconut oil. There were shrieks of laughter from Rita Bachan and Lily Kissoon. Mrs. Farley squeezed his ear until he was bent double against her, the blood filling his face, and he groaned in pain, unashamedly, begging her to stop. She let go of him abruptly and he held his ear and wept in pain and shame. That seemed to get rid of some of Mrs. Farley's anger. Now she walked along the queues again, her eyes daring them to laugh or joke. She looked each student in the eye as she passed them, studying their expression. June avoided her eyes. Merle Searwar was standing in front of June, she turned to look at Mrs. Farley's back and there was contempt in her eyes. June felt sure Mrs. Farley would not dare lay a hand on children like Merle, or Louise Sampson or Peter Johnson whose parents were above Mrs. Farley's station. If one of them had giggled she would not have dared to screw their ears. She wondered if it was the reason for Mrs. Farley's frustration, that her station in life was beneath so many of her students?

When Mrs. Farley decided to end her inspection of the queue she stopped and said to one of the boys, 'So you, Frank Hussein, have come to school for an education I see.'

Frank Hussein was one of the boys Rita Bachan had engaged in a running argument yesterday about the worth of his father's job as a chauffeur for one of the lawyers. Her own father owned a fleet of taxis. Frank stepped out of the queue and saluted smartly to shrieks of hilarity from Rita and Lily. He answered snappily, 'Yes Ma'am.'

Lily remarked, 'You, Frank Hussein, too stupid.'

He sucked his teeth, turned to her and said, 'Shut up.'

Before he could turn back to Mrs. Farley she lifted the cane and brought it down on his thigh. His right hand flew to shield his thigh and she brought the cane down on the hand. When he rubbed his right hand with his left hand she thrashed his left hand twice. He shrunk from her and she whipped him across his back freely. June turned to look around the compound, to see if anyone was watching, and saw Mr. Singh watching from the doorway of the auditorium. Frank took a few steps along the queue, backing away from Mrs. Farley but she pursued him, and whipped him with surprising strength and vigour, with a practised rhythm. Frank decided not to run and stood his ground, taking the lashes, his body jumping each time the cane made contact with his flesh. When she finished with him she strode to the front of the queue where Rabindranauth was still standing, took hold of his right wrist firmly and began to whip him as hard as she had whipped Frank. Rabindranauth was not as brave as Frank and his degradation was painful to watch. He threw himself on the stairs, lay there, then rolled around, writhed, groaned and wept loudly as he was beaten. It made it worse that his voice had broken and he sounded like a man, half-man, half-animal, in his agony. June turned to look at Rita Bachan accusingly and Rita returned a look emptied of feeling.

Mrs. Farley stopped whipping Rabindranauth and ordered him to rejoin the queue. He crawled from her in fear, sobbing and groaning, and took his place again. She shook her cane at them and asked if any of them wanted some of the same thing. She looked at each of them in turn, the cane held up in the air. She had shown what she could do, now she led them upstairs.

There was a heavy silence in the classroom while Mrs. Farley took the register. Lavender arrived and Mrs. Farley ordered her to go and wait in the auditorium. After the register Mrs. Farley made an angry speech which repeated Mr. Singh's. When she finished she told them that Mrs. Baxter would arrive soon to take them for mathematics and Mr. Doodnauth next door would keep an ear out for any mischief-makers and report them to her. She said that Miss Lewis had told her about their behaviour yesterday and they were clearly a class which needed teaching a special lesson. As June listened, her feelings of injustice grew. It was not fair, no justice had been done, the person who started the trouble was Rita Bachan, laughing at poor people, and it was poor people who got the punishment, because Mrs. Farley did not dare lay a hand on Rita. All Mrs. Farley could do was demonstrate her power, and pick on poor people to do it. There was no justice in this school, only madness.

Mrs. Farley left and there was nothing to say or do but wait for Mrs. Baxter to arrive. Rabindranauth was sitting with his head buried in his arms. He was weeping pitifully, rubbing the welts on his naked, hairy legs and arms. Cynthia Simmonds sat next to him, looking at him helplessly.

Merle commented, 'Mrs. Farley is a brute, that woman. When my brother was in the sixth form she tried to beat him and my father came in and told her never to lay a hand on any of us.'

'Where is your brother now?' June asked.

'He works with my father. Mrs. Farley thinks education is so important, but how could anybody get a good education in a place like this?'

Now Lavender returned to the classroom in tears, rubbing herself. Mrs. Farley had whipped her too. June left her seat and went to Lavender. Lavender was lying across her desk. She touched her on the shoulder and asked what happened. Lavender raised herself and showed June the welts which were beginning to rise along the inside of her arms. Annie Beardsley stared at Lavender's welts. Lavender declared that she was not staying in this school and got up to leave. It was then that Mrs. Baxter arrived; she glared at June and Lavender and ordered June back to her seat. She demanded to know why Lavender was leaving and Lavender declared that she was not staying there to be beaten like a mule.

'Who beat you?' Mrs. Baxter demanded.

'That old lady.'

Peter Johnson said, 'Mrs. Farley.'

Mrs. Baxter sighed and went to her desk. She put down her books and cleaned the blackboard. She turned to Lavender.

'Sit down, child, and come and see me afterwards. You are not to leave on any account or you will not be allowed back and your fees will not be refunded.' She turned to June. 'You, child, what is your name?'

'June Lehall.'

She turned to Lavender. 'And your name?'

'Lavender Jones.'

'Are you both from the country?'

There were sniggers from the class and Rita Bachan muttered, 'Country bacoos.'

'What does your father do?' Mrs. Baxter asked June.

'He is a mechanic.'

There were more sniggers from the class and Rita muttered, 'Grease monkey.'

'Does he work at home?'

'No Miss.'

'Don't call me *Miss,* I am *Mrs.* And you, Lavender Jones, I don't expect your parents are at home either. Do they work?'

Lavender answered rudely that she was not telling anybody what her parents did for them to laugh at them, but she told them by saying that it was a useful thing to be a guttersmith and a servant in the country; it was better than working in the canefields and the factory; guttersmiths and servants and mechanics had more freedom than pieceworkers.

There was so much laughter in the classroom not even Mrs. Baxter's cold stare could silence them. She had to snap very sharply, 'Be quiet!' before they stopped. She gave them all her coldest stare and declared that they were only revealing their ignorance, but then she snapped at Lavender too, 'Do you usually speak on a subject you are not requested to speak on? Do you not learn manners at home? It is clear not one of you have any manners. Now look here, Lavender Jones, it is up to you whether you desire an education or not but it is my responsibility to keep you here at least during this lesson. Do what you like after that. Stand at the back of the class. You are an extremely rude child.'

Mr. Sylvester followed Mrs. Baxter, then there were prayers in the auditorium. They were not allowed recess because of their behaviour yesterday. There was a history class with Miss Lewis, then the lunch break.

All the town children left for their homes, only the country children remained in the classroom. The girls went away in a group to look for a shady spot outdoors, the boys grouped together at the back of the class. June was about to join the other girls outside when she saw Lavender still sitting at her desk. She went to sit beside her. Soon, the boys began to throw around remarks about girls and it was not long before they were shouting about 'black pudding ladies' at the tops of their voices. When Lavender could not bear it any more she rounded on them and yelled 'Coolies! Coolie-water-rice!'

'Black pudding lady!' they shrieked back, and began throwing their books at her, African and Indian boys alike.

Lavender ran to the back of the class and got hold of Winston Franklin who was from Manchester Village on the Corentyne and began to kick him. June ran to Lavender, grabbed her blouse and tried to pull her away. Somar Guruwar took up a ruler and began to strike Lavender with it. They all lost their footing and crashed to the floor, Winston falling on top of Somar. Lavender was up first, she picked up a chair and threw it at the boys. This incensed them and they attacked her as one, Ronald King, Winston, Somar, and three others, pushing her towards the door then shoving her down the stairs. Lavender rolled halfway down, picked herself up then ran away. The boys regrouped round their tables.

June ran from the classroom too, but Lavender was nowhere to be found in the school grounds. Rather than hang around by herself, she decided to ride into New Amsterdam and look around the town. She felt too sick to be really interested, but rode through the very wide Main Street, past the large Dutch houses with their large jalousies, and the large shops filled with bolts of cloth and bright fluorescent lights. She rode as far as she could, until the road narrowed and branched into three. She turned left and cycled along the narrow street which led to a cul-de-sac and a wooden house which was as large as the Beardsleys' but had none of its yard space. There were verandahs round the house, on both storeys, and on the lower verandah sat Merle Searwar, who caught sight of her, called out her name and told her to come upstairs. Merle ran down the stairs and opened the large gates to let her in.

On the verandah there were several couches thick with cushions, and tables covered with linen tablecloths and ornaments. A large glass door separated the verandah from a living room which was just like the Beardsleys, filled with comfortable furniture, large mirrors on the wall, and paintings and photographs. Here the photographs were enlarged portraits of the Searwar family. June looked at each photograph and Merle explained each person's relation to her family. Merle's sister was a doctor. There were uncles, aunts and cousins who were doctors, lawyers and engineers.

June asked, 'You want to be a doctor too?'

Merle laughed and shrugged. 'I don't know what I want to be.'

Her answer shocked June – here was a rich child who could do anything she wanted and didn't know what she wanted to do. Merle smiled and asked her if she knew, and June had to confess that she did not know either. Merle kept on smiling and it began to get on June's nerves; it seemed that rich people did not have to try very hard to find country people funny.

She snapped at Merle, 'What you smiling about?'

Merle laughed loud. 'You really funny you know. I never met anybody with an inferiority complex like you. You quick to get vex!'

'And people like you quick to ridicule people.'

'I never ridiculed you!'

'I never want to come to this school you know.'

'And if you don't, what you will do? Cut cane? Marry a canecutter?'

'What wrong with cutting cane? If people didn't cut cane this country wouldn't exist.'

Merle laughed loudly again. 'What about bauxite? Rice? Timber? Fish? You think that King Sugar rule this country still? You living behind God back, that's why you don't know that this country is changing all the time.'

115

'Show off!'

'Anything I tell you, you will say I showing off.' Merle shrugged, sat down, gazed up at the sky and began to sing to herself.

June leaned against the verandah and stared down at the bougainvillaea bushes, brooding. 'How you know that sugar not important any more?'

'My father said so. He used to own a sugar plantation but he gave it up. He says Europe will grow their own sugar from beet and will have no use for West Indian sugar. He says we have to learn to do other things, not just grow sugar.'

Merle did not realise the effect she was having on June, and June could see she was not saying it out of spite. So Lucille was talking sense all this time, there was really no future on the sugar estates. What about Cyrus and Boysie and Mr. Easen? Did they really know nothing at all? Was Lucille right about them, that they were men who knew nothing? June felt crushed. One blow after another was being struck against New Dam, against everything she was. Why did Boysie bother to fight against the plantation if they were going to go anyway? June looked around her, at this house filled with luxury. How did she come to be here? It was better to stay in New Dam; she knew she should never have left. All the things she saw and heard were turning her against herself, making her own people look like nothing. It made it worse that Merle Searwar was not saying it to spite her. She wished Merle was as vicious as Rita Bachan instead of trying to make friends with her, playing nice. June decided not to go back to school, she would go straight home and tell Lucille she wanted to stay in New Dam and live there the rest of her life, no matter how bad things got. She would tell Lucille to let Mr. Easen, Cyrus and Boysie hold their meetings at the house and plan their village council, plan how to live without the sugar plantation.

Now Merle's mother came to the verandah with a tray of drink and cakes; June recognised her from the photograph on the wall. Merle introduced them and Mrs. Searwar shook her hand, showing the dimples in her cheeks like Merle's when she smiled. Merle told her mother that June was from New

Dam and Mrs. Searwar began to talk about her childhood on the Corentyne. She spoke affectionately about missing the community feeling, the peace, although she looked very happy here in her house; she said Merle had told her how Rita Bachan and her friends behaved and June was not to take them seriously, they were just ignorant children. She said she hoped June and Merle would be friends as both their families were Hindu and Christian and there was no reason the two should not blend well except that it seemed to cause a lot of destructive behaviour in some people who felt they had to look down on one or the other. She said there was a lot of racial misunderstanding in the country, but education could solve the problem. For example, Hindus were not backward and superstitious – she herself practised yoga and meditation and found it very satisfying spiritually; the Caribbean was a multiracial place, it was important to respect each other's cultures.

When Mrs. Searwar was finished speaking, June asked to be excused; she explained that she had to go home.

'What about school?' Merle asked. 'You will be late for school.'

'I don't want to go to school,' June shouted, and ran down the stairs to her bicycle.

She let herself out and cycled away without closing the gate after her, afraid that if she paused they would stop her. She did not look to her left or right. She rode as fast as she could through the town, as if she were being chased, and did not relax until she reached the open highway and the horizon of New Amsterdam began to shrink behind her.

All the way home she told herself this was the best thing she had done for a long time; it gave her the first feeling of justice. She felt so comfortable with herself she did not bother to put on her Panama hat, she just let the sun blaze down on her and enjoyed the heat, but when she reached the Welfare Club and the overseers houses appeared she began to worry about the effect it would have on Lucille and the baby she was expecting. It might make her sick. Her legs slowed on the pedals. Perhaps she should turn back and return to school. She stopped at the culvert near the Beardsleys' house, just behind the sentry

117

house which was empty. She sat on the wall and stared down at the disused canal. Perhaps she could hide under the bridge, with her bicycle, until four o'clock, then return home and pretend she had been to school, then she would go to school tomorrow. Quickly, she took the bicycle down the steep grassy slope but halfway down Sarah Beardsley appeared at the fence. June ignored her and continued down.

'What're you doing?' Sarah demanded.

'Mind your own damn business!'

'I will tell the guard. He will chase you away.'

'I got to hide here till four o' clock. Don' tell anybody.'

'Let me hide with you!'

'No, your mother will come to look for you.'

'My mother sleeps every afternoon until four o'clock, and I am left to do what I want.'

'What about the servants? They will look for you.'

'No, they let me run about the garden until four, then I have to go in and shower and change and do my piano.'

'Awright, come, but leave your bike, and behave yourself, don't give me any of your rudeness. I am bigger than you. You understand?'

Sarah nodded eagerly, hid her bicycle behind a shrub, let herself out and joined June on the slope. At that moment, Ralph Brijlall, her friend from St. Peter's, appeared on the bridge.

'Ai Muluk, whe' you going?' Ralph yelled.

He was wearing his canecutter's rags, caked in mud, his shirt knotted, pitchfork and saucepan across his shoulder, cutlass in his hand.

She felt stupid now. 'Go 'way Ralph, you can' see I doin' something?'

His face fell. 'Wha' you doin'? Why you goin' under culvert? You hidin'? You suppose to be at school.'

She sucked her teeth, annoyed with him. 'You proper like mind people business. And you 'in suppose to be at work too?'

'I been doin' piecework, man. I goin' home now. Come le' we go home. You don' want security catch y'u he', is real trouble-in-Arima you would get in. Come!'

He dropped his pitchfork, cutlass and saucepan and ran down the slope. He tried to take the bicycle from her and she resisted, but he was stronger. He rolled the bicycle up the slope to the bridge. She berated him, demanding to have her bicycle back. He laughed and coaxed her to come to the road and go home with him. She became angry and began to pelt him with the bricks which lined the canal. He laughed loudly and danced away from the bricks, telling her to practice more for a better aim. All this time, Sarah stood against the fence, looking on. June soon tired of pelting him and climbed up the slope. She took her bicycle from him and began to walk with him towards New Dam village.

Sarah yelled at them, 'Coolies!'

June turned around to see her looking angry and lonely. Ralph sucked his teeth loudly, stooped, picked up a stone from the roadside and threw it hard at Sarah. It fell against the fence, only a foot from her. Sarah screamed loudly, then she screamed again and again.

June slapped Ralph, 'You stupid fool! Why you pelt her?'

Ralph yelled at Sarah, 'Who you calling coolie? Don' call me coolie, you hear?' He picked up another stone and threw it but June pushed him and the stone fell into the canal.

Now Sarah was shaking and trembling and crying. June shouted, 'Go home, move, go to the gate. Go home.' Now the security guard was running towards them; he was coming from the house, yelling and shaking his fist at them.

Ralph shoved his saucepan, pitchfork and cutlass into her hands, ordered her to get on the carrier, fast, and cycled at speed towards the high bridge. He cycled recklessly, not sitting on the seat, leaning hard over the handlebars and pumping the pedals with all his strength. When they reached the high-bridge, he stopped on the downward slope, jumped off, and together they lifted the bicycle and ran under the bridge to hide on the narrow south bank of the canal, the water lapping at their feet. Ralph put his finger to his lips, signalling her to be silent. There was no sound on the road, and they sat on the concrete beam to wait.

'Why you had to stone her?' She asked.

He sucked his teeth and avoided her eyes. He looked mean now, don't-care-a-damn. 'She 'in call me coolie? You 'in hear?

Or town school tek 'way y'u ears?' He grinned. 'I like y'u uniform, man. You look like real police now, serge blue, leather shoes an' t'ing.' He laughed, amused.

She sighed. 'I don' like the school at all.'

'What? You tell y'u mammy so?'

'I not going back.'

He shook his finger at her, 'You try!'

She teased him. 'You wearin' uniform too.'

He smiled half-heartedly, took up the cutlass and began to scrape the mud from his heels. 'Uniform? dis? Hmp! Dis 'in uniform, girl, dis is me grave I wearin', me coffin. Dis is wha' we gon all end up in, good Guiana mud, me, you, governor, prime minister, lawyer, overseer. Dust to dust.' He was grim like a man, but he smiled quickly, and threw a handful of mud at her.

She threw back a handful of mud at him; it splattered his face. He ran to the water and washed his face, laughing, then he began to whip palmfuls of water towards her, creating a spray which drenched her. He threw back his head and laughed to see her dripping wet. She ran to him and pushed him into the canal. They laughed until they could not laugh any more and he climbed out of the canal and came to sit beside her, cleaned of mud. Calmer, they talked about their new lives, he about work in the canefields, she about the new school, listening to each other without comment.

When they were almost dry they left the bridge and began to walk home. When she told him what Merle Searwar had said, he commented, 'Sugar plantation will finish yes, but not how people expect. It won' come by big politics like British versus Jagan or even by l'il politics like Boysie versus overseer. Different trouble coming.'

'What kind trouble coming?'

He shrugged. 'Trouble always coming.'

'Like you like trouble bad nowadays. Sugar estate work turning you hard. You always used to be the one who would stop children fighting at school, you would stop everybody from fighting. Now all you want to do is fight.'

He sucked his teeth. 'White people don' care 'bout we, an'

night an' day we growin' they blasted sugar, lookin' after they property.'

White people, white people, they were in his blood now. She asked him again, 'What kind trouble coming?'

'You would jus' talk, man.'

'Who I would talk to?'

'The same white girl I jus' see you with, Beardsley daughter. You t'ink I 'in notice how she want play with you? You going to big shot school now, man. You like white people now.'

'She is a child. She don't understand nothing at all. She would say anything to make anybody notice she.'

'She understand very well. I see how good she listen when we talk. Tha's why I pelt she.'

'You talkin' pure stupidness. You know very well Overseer Beardsley is the one good overseer on the compound.'

'Well, if I talkin' stupidness don' ask me no more question.'

'Tell me about this trouble that coming.'

They were passing the Anglican church now. He threw a brick at the jumbie tree. 'Plenty men 'in get no bonus pay this month. It does affect them bad. One man kill he'self, a fellow from Cumberland.'

'Because he didn't get bonus pay he kill himself?'

'He had other worries, but he work for he bonus and they 'in give he none. Look girl, you don' know how much trouble plantation work is.'

'Tha's why you all going on strike? How come Boysie don't know about it? He was at our house last night and he didn't say anything.'

'Boysie is small fish now. He politics belong to old days, ancient days. Overseer don' frighten Boysie no more. They frighten Jagan, communist. Tha's why they send soldier and when people see soldier they come to feel, well, Jagan is the real strong man, make overseer shit brick.'

'Yes, but Boysie say you all don't know what you fighting for any more. You just fighting for the sake of fighting, out of desperation, with no rhyme and reason.'

He sucked his teeth, and said provocatively. 'But bonus 'in the only reason we goin' strike. Plenty other reason too.'

'Like what?'

'You too fast you know.' He was enjoying her curiosity. 'You is spy or what? Boysie say you father is spy, that he does tell Overseer Beardsley we secrets.'

'Sometimes Boysie ruction bad. Is Mother he don't like because she is Christian and for that reason he like to provoke Father.' She persisted. 'So what, you mean to say you don' belong to Boysie union?'

He nodded. 'We formin' new union, and the first thing we going do is kill Overseer Johnson, kill he dead.'

'What Overseer Johnson do you?'

He looked guilty. They were outside her cottage now.

Her mother sat at the window, at her sewing machine, and beside her sat Savitri Ramessar and Rachael Jones.

'Come inside,' June invited him.

He was walking to the gate with her but Lucille shouted from the window. 'June, you are to come in alone!'

Before she could protest Ralph turned and ran down the road. June climbed the stairs alone.

Indoors, Rachael exclaimed, 'My goodness, look at the terrible state of your nice uniform!'

Savitri commented, 'Plenty of pleats to press. I hope you good with the hot iron. You will have to get it nice and clean for school tomorrow!'

The thought of returning to school made her feel ill, and she was angry with Lucille for sending Ralph away. She declared. 'I not going back to no school!'

All three women looked surprised. Lucille asked, 'What you said?'

June did not feel afraid. She felt determined. 'I am not going back to no school!'

Lucille asked, 'If you don't go back to school what will you do here in New Dam? Work in the canefields, manuring and giving the men water? Milking the cows at the dairy? Bailing punts? Weeding canals? You want to be like Mariam Motoo?'

June snapped, 'Yes! Yes! It better than New Amsterdam children! All they go to school to do is 'buse down one another. They not interested in studying one little bit. At lessons today they didn't know anything and the teachers don't dare criticise them so we country children take all the blame! Only 'busing down, insulting and beating go on at that school!'

Lucille lost her composure. 'All right! Stay at home then! Turn into a coolie! You used to be a coolie and I manage to turn you into a civilised person, now you want to turn coolie again!'

June declared passionately, 'I will go and live with Nani.'

Lucille looked angry and hurt. Savitri said, 'She don't know what she saying, Lucille. Let her cool down.'

Lucille hissed, 'Yes, go and live with Dharamdai and all the cowdung she puts in her bottomhouse!'

June hissed back, 'Nothing wrong with cowdung. Nani says the cow is sacred, and too besides, it keeps the earth from cracking up like Mr. Easen's yard.'

Lucille hissed, 'Stupid girl! You believe all that ignorance she tells you? That illiterate woman who can't speak English?'

'Is not ignorance! Nani not ignorant!'

Lucille shrieked, 'All right! Go! Go then! I will disown you! You go and live with your mati coolie!'

All June's pain exploded and she began to sob. Rachael hugged her and Savitri put her arm round Lucille, but June tore herself from Rachael's arms, ran downstairs, into the wooden shell of the new lavatory, and locked herself in, bolting the door firmly. She sat down and howled out her grief and torment freely.

The women followed her downstairs. Lucille banged on the door. Savitri pleaded with Lucille to leave her alone but Lucille shouted, 'Come out at once!' When June only continued to sob, she launched a tirade of resentment at her. 'All my life I try to bring you up decently but you want to be a coolie! That Dharamdai hounding us with her coolie ways, telling me to say mantras and do puja. Next thing you know she will make marriage match for you to marry an Indian! Yes, you marry one!' Rachael and Savitri pleaded with Lucille not to go so far but she ignored them. 'Yes, you marry a coolie! You see their weddings? How loud and vulgar they are? What they know about India or Indian customs in this place? They should try and improve their lives instead of bothering with Indian

123

customs! It is all hypocrisy! Look how the men behave! They love to boast about being Hindu, how they are better than creoles! And what is the truth? The truth is they go to the whorehouses in Pitt Street in New Amsterdam!'

Rachael pleaded, 'Lucille calm yourself. Both you and June are in a hysterical state. You are making it worse. She doesn't understand the things you are talking about. For heaven's sake.'

Lucille ranted on. '...they drink rum, they just eat and drink rum in their spare time, and beat their wives, and fight at the rumshops and the weddings. You like that coolie boy Ralph Brijlall? You like him? Well marry him and see if you still like him when he is finished with you! Their wives cook from three o' clock in the morning to late at night! You want to be a coolie woman? Well be a coolie woman! I don't care! Coolie women have to carry all the burdens for the men, the burden of the sick, the old, the children, burying the dead, and get no thanks for it, only licks! And the women beat their daughters and treat them worse than the men treat them! I don't beat you! And what do I get for it? Ingratitude! Ingrate! Yes, you go to Dharamdai's house. You talk Hindi, learn mantras, do puja, pick up cow dung with your hands, bring up children with lice in their hair and feed the lice with coconut oil! You see if it will get you anywhere in this country! This is the West Indies, not India, not Africa, not China, the West Indies! We are British!'

Savitri was shouting at the top of her voice now. 'Lucille think of the child you are carrying. You will do yourself a terrible damage if you don't calm down right now. I don't know what Cyrus will say. Why you letting a little child excite your passion so?'

Now June shouted back at her mother. 'You talk as if Indian people poor because of their own fault! Is not their fault! They work hard! Not all Indian people poor and stupid. You will find poor people in England too! You think white people are Gods! Nani poor but she not stupid at all. She have more sense than you!'

Now Lucille began to sob. She shouted. 'You are a wicked wicked girl! God will punish you!'

The door was bolted so firmly, the wood was so strong and new, June felt able to speak out all her anger now. She declared, 'Which god? I don't have no god so no god can't punish me. And I don't have no mother either. You can't do me anything,' After she said this she did not feel the triumph, the sense of victory she expected to feel. She only felt sicker than she had felt before. She listened for her mother's response but the women were taking Lucille upstairs, and she was weeping.

After a few minutes she began to regret everything she had said. The feeling of sickness was spreading all over her body, from her head to her toes. She felt suffocated by the smell of new wood. She could hear the footsteps upstairs as the women made drinks in the kitchen. She could hear them in the bedroom. They were putting Lucille to bed. She did not feel able to go to Lucille. The feeling of nausea began to go hard in her stomach, growing bigger and bigger until she felt she had to get out and get fresh air into her lungs. She slipped the bolt and ran out of the yard and on to the public road. There were people on the road, men for the night shift at the factory. Nana Bissoondyal, Nani's husband, would be among them. Nani would be alone at home. She would go there. She ran all the way to Lot No. 50 on the other side of New Dam.

11 OBLATION

Nani's cottage faced the canefields where the breeze blew freely, ruffling the cane sheaves and rippling the red triangular flag at her gate. By the time June reached the gate, the red of the flag seemed to match the heat of the fever in her body and thoughts. Nani was not as Lucille said; Nani kept a lawn which was as good as the overseers'; there were covered water barrels in each corner of her yard and she always boiled her water for drinking and cooking; there was not a plank of rotting wood on the cottage, the bridge, the gate or paling staves; the cottage was painted fresh white, the zinc roof bright red; the bottomhouse was daubed and swept regularly; the curtains, doormat, sugarsack hammocks and rugs were always clean; the yard was always richly perfumed with the scents of the lime and hibiscus trees along the fence; this was a Hindu's cottage and there was nothing wrong with it, nothing dirty or backward, which was all she had heard about since she started going to that school in New Amsterdam. Lucille, who should know better, said those things too, because she tried so hard to be Christian and it was too hard for her. When she let herself cry, the tears burnt her flesh. Her flesh was hot but she felt cold, exposed in the warm breeze. She opened the gate and ran up the front stairs.

Inside the cottage, Nani was sitting on a *pirahi*. Her long grey hair was loose over her shoulders and she was combing it patiently. When she looked up and saw June, with her skin flushed, shivering, her face dirty with tears and sweat, her shoulders heaving with repressed sobs, she exclaimed, '*Aray bapray, Muluk!'* and continued in Hindi, opening her arms and beckoning her to approach. In Nani's arms her tears dried and her tension eased. Nani rocked her like a baby, muttering on

126

in Hindi, commenting in English occasionally: 'Fever, Muluk gat fever.'

Nani took her to the bedroom and laid her on the coconut sacking there. She covered her in a blanket and sheet. The room smelt of camphor and coconut oil. There was a *bedi* in the corner of the room, facing east, and a picture of Ram and Sita on the wall. She fetched a large drink of fresh coconut water from the kitchen which she made her drink, and a bottle of coconut oil. She helped June take off the uniform, then bathed her hair in the oil. She laid her on her stomach and massaged her, then on her back and massaged her again, praying in Hindi all the while: '*Aum bam asi astu. Aum...*' June remembered this prayer. It was for *havan*. It meant, 'Let my tongue speak, ears hear, nose inhale, eyes see, arms and thighs be strong, let all the limbs be strong.' As she prayed, Nani touched each part of the body the prayer referred to. When she finished the massage, she dressed her in a clean vest and a large shirt, then covered her again, telling her to go to sleep, then she went to the *bedi,* took the camphor, lit it, and began to recite the mantra for the ritual. June listened to the words, remembering their meaning now: *These three worlds are as vast as the sky and they are to be regarded as mother earth. I ignite the fire on this altar on this earth.* Nani fanned the fire with her hand while she recited this mantra. She said the next mantra then threw three pieces of bel wood, one by one, into the fire, after dipping them in ghee. She said a mantra for each piece of bel wood: *O fire, accept this piece of wood, light it and bless us and give us children, livestock, holiness and food.* Next she made an offering of ghee and sprinkled water on each side of the *bedi* after she spoke the mantra: *Let the gods of speech purify our words... let the sun grace this sacrifice, its worshippers, let the gods grace us, let the gods of speech sanctify our tongue.*

The burning wood, ghee and camphor were meant to have healing powers, to purify the atmosphere, like the incense at the Anglican church – it was no different. The scents filled the room and the memory of her quarrel with Lucille vanished. Nani's prayers lulled her to sleep.

She dreamt about her Christian baptism. It was like the baptism she had seen. She was a baby (as in her photographs),

127

Father Brown (he was in the photographs too) was holding her over the font in the church. He prayed and poured water over her head and smiled although she cried. The church was filled with the scent of candles, incense, wine, and the musky smell of the jumbie trees where the huge calabashes grew.

When she woke from this dream, it was dark and Nani was sitting beside her. Her lined face broke into a smile and she said, 'Jago!' She felt June's forehead and spoke in Creolese. 'Fever die down. You feel alright?' June nodded. 'You been arguin' in y'u sleep.'

June asked for water. Nani went to the kitchen and returned with water and a bowl of dhal which June drank up quickly. When she was finished, Nani told her there was a puja prayer which children should recite when they are ill. She made her repeat the prayer after her. After this prayer, Nani began to question her.

'Wha' happen beti? Why you been cry so?'

June talked about her quarrel with Lucille. Nani shook her head as she listened. When she finished, Nani said, 'Vijay (this was Lucille's name which only Nani used) never say mantra when you start school, that is why your soul disturb.'

She shook her head and sighed, then began to recount Lucille's and Cyrus's family history to June. Her Chinese name was Li-Hau but the immigration officer could not spell it and wrote it 'Lehall'. This had happened to most of their names. It was important to remember your real name even if the overseers and government officials preferred to spell it how it suited them. People took Christian names to help them get jobs too, or when they converted to Christianity, sometimes just to get a job but sometimes because they believed in the Christian god, sometimes a mixture of the two – who was to judge, as long as we keep our souls pure; Lucille's real name was Vijay, and her grandfather had become a tailor and used to have a tailorshop at Palmyra; Lucille had two brothers, they had run away from the Christianity and one was in the lumber business at Kwakwani, the other worked at the control tower at Atkinson Airport; Lucille had taken their father's side against them, that was why they never came to New Dam.

Then Nani began to scold June: she must respect her mother no matter what she did or said, she was a good mother; we were in this world to live a good life. Hear my words, Nani concluded. She told June she would now send for her parents.

She brought a plate of hot roti, dhal and calaloo, told June to eat it, then went to the landing, called to one of the small boys in the street and asked him to fetch Lucille and Cyrus. Nani spoke in creolese but she used Hindi for her prayers, and when the creolese could not keep up with her feelings. She returned to the bedroom with her own dinner and sat on a *pirahi* and ate. She asked June to tell her about her new school, and listened to her without comment, only shaking her head occasionally. When she finished her meal she went to wash her hands and returned to sit beside her again.

When footsteps sounded on the stairs, Nani told her to stay in the bedroom until she was sent for, then she went to the landing to greet Lucille and Cyrus. June could hear their voices clearly.

Nani spoke in Hindi. To June's surprise, Cyrus replied in Hindi. He said, *'Apko dekane aya.'*

Lucille said, 'She is not an orphan.' Nani spoke in a voice too low for June to hear everything, then Lucille spoke again, 'She has a name – June. You must not call her "Muluk". You have been the cause of the whole village calling her "Muluk". "Muluk" is not a proper name for a child, not in Hindi or English.'

Nani became angry and snapped at Lucille, *'Achchi bat kaho!'* Nani spoke more Hindi.

June began to wonder whether Lucille understood Hindi; it seemed that she had some knowledge, though she heard Cyrus translating for her. 'She only says we must pray for June, we must look after her spiritual welfare.'

Lucille retorted angrily, 'What spiritual welfare? June does not like to go to church, she is not interested in god or prayers.'

Nani spoke in Hindi again, at great length.

Lucille snapped at her, 'Why don't you speak to me in English?'

Cyrus protested, 'She can't speak English so well. She can barely manage the creolese and she is not comfortable with it.'

129

Lucille insisted. 'She can speak creolese very well, and English. She is no fool. She is doing it to annoy me.'

Nani scolded Lucille, *'Chup raho!'*

Cyrus said, 'You are wrong, Lucille. You are upsetting her.'

Lucille quarrelled, 'I am not related to her. She must not call me "beti". June should not call her "nani", she is not her grandmother, and Bissoondyal is not her grandfather. June is not an orphan, she treats her like an orphan.'

Now Cyrus spoke to Nani at length in Hindi, and when he was finished, Nani returned to the bedroom.

In the bedroom she brought June's uniform out from the bundle under her bed where she kept clean clothes. She had dusted and ironed the uniform. *'Jamin se utho,'* she said. She helped June to dress, asking her, *'Tum kal karoge?'* When she was dressed, Nani stroked her hair and said, *'Ghar jao. Sada sukhi raho.'*

June met her parents on the landing. Cyrus shook his head at her and Lucille looked away angrily. There were children playing on the path. As they left Nani's yard, the children parted for them.

When they reached the public road Lucille began to complain again about how mischievous it was for Nani to call them by Indian names, to speak Hindi when she was capable of speaking Creolese, to encourage June at her house, and why had she bathed her in coconut oil, she had no right at all.

June defended Nani. Yes, Nani did understand English but it was difficult for her to speak it, it did not come to her tongue easily; she did not call them Indian names to make mischief but because they did have Indian names and she liked to use them, and she did not insult Christians – she gave Mr. Easen and Nurse Hindu pictures, not to insult them but for the sake of respecting each other's religions, and she did not encourage her at the house, she went of her own free choice.

Lucille grumbled, 'I send you to school to be educated, not to defy me.'

Cyrus supported June. 'Nani is not malicious. She feels she has an obligation to our parents to take an interest in us. It would not be natural if she did not feel that. They were friends.'

'I am no longer a child,' Lucille insisted. 'She treats me like a child. I am a grown woman. I cannot stand the way old Indian women treat younger women like children.'

Cyrus said. 'You have it all wrong, Lucille. You are making a bad mistake.'

'You shouldn't be taking her side, Cyrus. You are never at home. If you had been at home this afternoon, this would never have happened.'

Cyrus became angry, 'Tha's because I have to be working night and day to make money to pay for the school fees and lavatory. You even want me to buy a car!'

Lucille said nothing else and they walked the rest of the way home in silence.

At home, Cyrus sat with June at the table and told her there would be no discussion about whether or not she would go to New Amsterdam High School: tomorrow, she would go to school. He told her there might be a strike though, the road outside the factory would be full of demonstrators; it would not be safe for her to cycle past the factory. They had decided she should spend the night at the junior staff compound, with Savitri Ramessar and her husband, Leonard. She would be safer starting her journey to school from there.

12 THE KILLING OF MARIAM

When she woke up on the Morris chair in Savitri's cottage, she thought she was dreaming. Instead of bare painted zinc and rafters above, the zinc roof was blocked off by a painted wooden ceiling from which a lampshade dangled. There were frilly cotton curtains at the window. A radio was on in another room, a shower and a tap were running and there was more space, more light in this cottage. Was she dreaming of the future, that they were living in the cottage Lucille wanted, with running water, electricity, a radio that worked, and more space? In such a short space of time, she had crossed into so many other people's lives, it was possible the future had come at last, and the child she used to be, the one who went to St. Peter's Anglican School in Old Dam and knew nothing much about the outside world except hearsay – it was possible that child had never lived.

Savitri called, 'June, wake up, get ready for school!'

Leonard Ramessar came into the living room. 'Morning Muluk!' He had showered and was dressed, not in his factory khakis, but his house clothes – like the men when they worked night shifts. He stood before the wall-mirror and shaved, stopping sometimes to sharpen the razor on the leather belt round his neck.

Savitri called again. 'June, your uniform is in the bathroom. Go, shower and get dressed.'

In the bathroom, she turned on the tap and let the water flow through her fingers for a long time before she could use it. She turned on the shower and watched it rain into the tiled cubicle, afraid of the experience of bathing under it. A whole room just for a shower, lavatory and sink – Lucille's dream.

After her shower she went to the kitchen – a whole room for a kitchen too. There was an aluminium sink with a tap, a gas stove and a large refrigerator, and a suite of arborite table and chairs. She ate toast and fried eggs with Savitri.

'Savitri!' Leonard called, 'Savitri, come quick!'

She followed Savitri to the living room. Leonard pointed outside. Cane soot was raining outside. He led them to the bedroom. The window was open and soot was pouring through. He shut it quickly, then he and Savitri checked all the windows, bolting them tight.

Savitri said, 'Who burning cane?'

Leonard replied. 'Whoever it is will get into big trouble.' He went to the telephone near the front door and spoke to the factory manager who ordered him to turn out at the factory.

Savitri asked, 'Exactly what going on?'

He replied, 'They set fire to the biggest field. Is real trouble. Riot police coming from New Amsterdam, and the British soldiers turning out too.' He paused, then asked her, 'You heard any rumours yesterday?'

'Yes.'

'What you heard?'

'I hear it in New Dam.'

'Well, tell me, quick.'

'I not telling you. You will tell overseer.'

'Look woman, tell me what you hear.'

'Only if you promise not to tell overseer.'

'Awright, awright, I promise. Now tell me.'

'They say is the Brijlall boy, the biggest one, Sookdeo.' She was hesitating.

'Go on, woman, tell me.'

'He and his friends.'

'Well?'

'Something to do with Overseer Johnson.'

'Overseer Johnson courting the mother, Bibi Mahadeo.'

'Yes, and as if that wasn't bad enough, he is molesting Sookdeo's girlfriend, Yasmin, now, and the boy is up in arms. They say he is going to burn down Overseer Johnson house. They said they were going to do it during Boysie's strike over the bonus and say it was part of the strike.'

'These people!'

'Don't tell the overseer, or police, or army!'

'Why you don't stay here on the compound and mind your own business?'

'Stay here and play white lady whole day?'

'Why you didn't tell them not to mix up personal grudge and strike?'

'They would listen to me? They call me "coolie overseer". Now look, I only tell you so you would know how to handle yourself, not for you to go and play traitor.'

He sucked his teeth and left, telling her to stay indoors and keep all the doors and windows bolted. When he was gone, Savitri could not settle down to anything. She was restless and frightened. At first June could not imagine why she should be frightened, then she began to realise that it was because Savitri and Leonard were Christians. Savitri, Lucille, Rachael, Nurse and Mistress Sampson were the five leaders of the Mothers Union. Ordinarily, their religion was their own business, but now the workers and overseers were closing their ranks, where would the black Christians go?

June looked outside and saw the sky thick with soot which blew around like bats in the air. Many canefields were burning now, and burning fast. She helped Savitri sweep up the soot from the floor then sat with her as she worked at her sewing machine. By midday, the soot was thin in the air and it was possible to open a window. When Savitri looked outside, there was a large crowd at the main gate to the junior staff compound – all her neighbours had left their cottages and were gathered there. When she asked what was happening they told her that Overseer Johnson's house was burning, and pointed to the senior staff compound. A pall of black smoke was rising from one of the houses there. Savitri was told that punts had been sunk, the horses let out of the stables. June leaned from the window with Savitri. There was the sound of sirens in the air and a fire engine appeared near the Welfare Club. It sped past the crowd at the gate and turned into the senior staff compound. A second, then a third fire engine followed. Now the telephone was ringing in the cottage. Savitri ran to answer it.

It was Mistress Sampson on the telephone; she wanted to come to Savitri's house.

'Yes, yes, come and stay here,' Savitri said, and put down the receiver. She told June, 'The Sampsons coming over to stay here. She says workers are hiding in the canefields behind the compound. Those fields haven't been burnt. Mistress Sampson says she can hear them. They think a fire will start there. The police and soldiers might come in now. The men want Johnson and can't find him.'

Mistress Sampson arrived at the junior staff compound in her car. Louise was with her, so was Peter Johnson. The crowd parted to let them in, and she drove to the back of the cottage and parked there. Savitri led them in, without a sign of anxiety that the Johnson boy was among them. Mistress Sampson began to fuss so much, June escaped from the cottage.

June was halfway down the stairs when she saw the crowd of boys and men approach the main gate from the public road. Ralph and his brother, Sookdeo, were among them. They were carrying cutlasses, paling staves, pitchforks and sticks. When they reached the gate Sookdeo moved to the front of the crowd, struck the gate with his cutlass and demanded to know whether Overseer Johnson and his family were hiding here. He said that one of the servants told him Overseer Johnson was here. A woman in the crowd turned and pointed to June, saying that they were there, in the Ramessar cottage. The eyes of the crowd turned accusingly on her and she looked at Ralph who shouted up to her, 'Where Johnson?'

Sookdeo brandished his cutlass at her. 'You go home. You don' belong he', go!'

She did not move. She felt hypnotised. Someone opened the gate. The crowd entered and approached the stairs. They numbered only a dozen men, mostly young boys, probably Sookdeo's friends, but a bigger crowd was approaching on the public road now and they included men and women – Boysie and Mariam were leading them.

Ralph warned Sookdeo. 'Look Boysie and Mariam coming.'

Sookdeo ran up the stairs and began to kick the front door. Savitri, Mistress Sampson and Louise began to scream. Sookdeo began to scream abuse about Overseer Johnson.

June grabbed Ralph by the shirt. 'Overseer Johnson not here, only his son, a small boy.'

Ralph was so frightened, his eyes bulged. She could see his heart was not in it. It was Sookdeo's grudge.

Now Boysie, Mariam and the strikers formed a huge, noisy crowd at the public road. Boysie strode into the private compound, towards the cottage. He stopped at the bottom of the stairs and ordered Sookdeo to join the crowd. He said, 'This is a strike, I not concerned with you' quarrel with Overseer Johnson. Bring you' backside down he' before you give soldier and police good reason to kill we.'

The crowd became excited. They were pointing towards the high bridge. 'Look, police truck coming.'

Boysie ran back to the crowd. He ordered them to turn and face the police. 'An' don' let them think you frighten.'

Sookdeo descended the stairs slowly and made his way with his friends and Ralph into the crowd.

Someone pointed in the opposite direction, towards Lucius Village. 'Look, army comin' from Lucius side.'

A truckload of British soldiers was crossing the canal. The police truck arrived outside the cottage. It stopped a few yards from the strikers. Armed policemen in blue sat in the rear. There were two jeeploads of policemen behind the truck and they were also armed with rifles. Sergeant Richards, who manned the police station in Good Land, jumped from one of the jeeps and approached the crowd.

'Wha's all this?' the sergeant demanded.

Boysie declared, 'This is a union strike. The overseers know about it. They had warning.' Boysie laughed. 'So they send you plenty policemen with guns, Richards. You get plenty reinforcement.'

The sergeant pointed to the cottages. 'Why you stage your strike here, in a residential area?'

Mariam pointed towards the high bridge. 'We stage strike at factory but we come he' fo' collec' some o' we people.'

The sergeant gave Mariam and Boysie a distrustful look. He pointed to the senior staff compound. 'Any of you know anything about that fire?'

Boysie shook his head.

The sergeant said, 'Two big canefields and one overseer house burn down, and now you staging strike right in front the overseer quarters. How come you know nothing about it? You telling me is just coincidence?'

'You makin' accusation?' Boysie demanded.

Sergeant Richards shook his fingers at Boysie. 'You better don't provoke me, Boysie. I know you too good. You playing with real trouble today. You think you is Cheddi and Janet Jagan. If you want be politician go Georgetown and turn politician. We don't want politicians here. Now you all had better tell me who burn down Overseer Johnson house.'

Some people in the crowd protested that they were being wrongly accused.

The sergeant pointed to Sookdeo who was still carrying his cutlass. 'What cause you have to be armed?'

Sookdeo's friends had thrown their weapons into the deep drain and the grassy parapet concealed them, but he was still carrying his cutlass. A policeman came forward and whispered into the sergeant's ear. The Sergeant said 'Send him!' and the policeman opened the door of the truck to let out the man sitting near the driver. It was the security guard who worked for the Beardsleys, who had seen Ralph stone Sarah Beardsley. He pointed straight at Ralph. The sergeant nodded and the security guard returned to the truck.

Mariam screamed at the guard, 'You blasted coolie traitor you. You own mati you betray!'

The sergeant ordered Ralph, 'You come here.'

Ralph began to shake with fear. Sookdeo and Mariam moved to stand in front of him, blocking his way.

'What you want with he?' Sookdeo asked.

'Questioning. He is a suspect.'

Sookdeo shouted: 'Suspect? Suspect fo' wha'?'

Some of the policemen began to jump off the trucks and the crowd became restless. The policemen formed three lines and made their way, one line through the centre of the crowd, the other two flanking them. Three jeeploads of British soldiers were parked behind the crowd; they began to leave their jeeps too, making their way in two lines to the front of the crowd. One of the soldiers held a brief discussion with the sergeant, then spoke into a walkie-talkie which crackled and had a hypnotic effect on people in the crowd.

The sergeant spoke to Boysie. 'You should not be here in this private compound. You are trespassing; I could jail you all jus' for trespassing but instead I am ordering you all to disperse and go home or else I will start arresting.' He pointed to Ralph. 'All except this fella, the only one we have a witness for. He has to come in for questioning.'

Boysie demanded to know whether the sergeant had a warrant for Ralph's arrest.

'This is a riot. I don't need a warrant.'

'Riot? Where deh riot?' Boysie demanded.

'A house and two canefields burn. Men are hiding in the canefields and threatening to attack more private property on the plantation. You stand up here demonstrating in private compound and playing innocent with me, Boysie? I am telling you to tell your people to disperse right now and go home.

Some of the crowd were frightened and dispersed but they lingered in the distance to watch. Now the windows and doors of the cottages were crowded with spectators. In the senior staff compound, the verandahs of the houses were crowded with overseers and their families and servants. Boysie asked for permission for the workers to go to the factory and continue with their demonstration. The sergeant refused. Boysie accused him of working for the overseers, breaking up a peaceful demonstration. The sergeant laughed, turned to his men and ordered them to come forward and take in Ralph.

As the policemen approached, Sookdeo rushed at them, brandishing his cutlass. Mariam grabbed his shirt and pulled him back so violently he fell against Ralph. The guns went off and Mariam, Sookdeo and Ralph fell together to the ground. Pandemonium broke out. The air rang with screams and hoarse shouts. The rifles of the policemen and soldiers were raised and pointed all around, at everyone, including the cottages where children sat on the landings and stairs.

Ralph began to groan with shock and grief, as if he had been

138

shot, and women began to wail and scream. Most of the strikers had thrown themselves to the ground when the shots rang out and some remained crouched there. Boysie still stood his ground but he looked sick and frightened. All the violence of his feelings had broken through the surface and the reality sickened him. No one dared to move. The screams of the women were dying now. The sergeant, his voice loud, but hoarse with tension, ordered the crowd to disperse, and the people in the cottages to go indoors and shut themselves in. They obeyed him, and the men began to walk towards their villages. Mistress Sampson emerged from the cottage and led June indoors.

In the cottage, Louise, Peter and Savitri were weeping. Mistress Sampson began to pray. June opened a window slightly and heard the walkie-talkie crackle into life. A British soldier was asking for an ambulance to be sent from New Amsterdam, but someone had already phoned New Amsterdam for one. Sirens sounded, followed by the noise of sharp braking. Now men were arguing, Boysie among them. Savitri and Mistress Sampson joined June at the window and peered outside. Sookdeo was walking into the ambulance. Ralph was being put into the police jeep. Mariam was being put on a stretcher, her body covered from head to toe.

Mistress Sampson crossed herself and said, 'Poor woman. God help us...'

The sirens sounded again and the ambulance drove away towards New Amsterdam. Boysie was shouting, telling his men to go to the bridge and demonstrate. His voice was angry. The crowd gathered again. Three jeeps of soldiers and policemen had left but the others were still there, pointing their guns. Gunfire rang out. In the cottage they crouched down under the window. Mistress Sampson peered outside and said they were firing into the air now, people were running away. Sounds of the struggle reached them. Men were shouting their defiance hoarsely. They could hear the voices of the policemen and soldiers too. The motors of the jeeps and trucks fired, there was the screech of tyres and the sound of them driving away.

139

13 THE FUNERAL

Now, Boysie was the natural leader, with New Dam awaiting retribution from the overseers and the governor in Georgetown. He wanted to make sure that Mariam had an honourable funeral but during the two days following her killing he was busy giving morale-boosting public speeches at the roadside in Lucius, Pheasant and Good Land villages. He reminded them that in 1912, another worker had been shot dead at Old Dam high bridge; it showed that nothing had changed, Georgetown still did not understand the grievances of plantation people; they sent policemen and soldiers to kill them the minute they complained; they engineered a disaster like Mariam's killing which put estate people in the world spotlight as savages, yet it was estates like New Dam which made money and none of it, not a black cent, came back to New Dam so why should they be afraid now of the governor and the legislative assembly in Georgetown, the army, the police, and the British and American governments; let the radio station in England broadcast how violent Guiana estate workers were and how England had to send troops; let all the newspapers in the world print it – it was all lies; the important thing was for the estate workers themselves to understand their position, to know that justice was on their side. He urged them to buy the newspapers and be aware of what was happening in Georgetown. Georgetown and the rural areas were at war now. Remember, he warned, that on Thursday, October 8th, 1953 British troops had invaded the country because a Labour Relations Bill which would give sugar workers the freedom to join the union of their choice had been passed. He declared Mariam the latest martyr of their fight for liberation. He urged everyone to attend her funeral and demonstrate their fighting spirit to Georgetown – the newspaper reporters would be there.

On the day Mariam's corpse was returned to New Dam there was no warning of its arrival, only the appearance of the New Amsterdam hearse on the public road, in the hot, blazing midday sun. June was sitting on the landing and saw the hearse cross the bridge, then stop.

The driver yelled up to her, 'Where Lot No. 39?'

She ran to the public road to tell him, then asked 'That is Mariam in the coffin?'

He nodded and drove off. She ran upstairs again to get her shoes. While she was putting them on, Lucille, who was resting in bed, called to her: 'June, what is going on. You are not allowed to leave the village, there is an emergency situation on the estate.' She shouted her explanation from the door: she was going to Mariam's cottage, the hearse was there. Lucille ordered her not to go but she did not listen.

By the time June reached Lot No. 39, the news had spread and people were beginning to leave their cottages too. Nani Dharamdai was already at the cottage. She was wearing her ornhi and prayed in Hindi over the coffin as it was lifted from the hearse by the driver and Mariam's brothers. Water dripped from the coffin. As she prayed, Nani sprinkled the coffin with water from her *lota*. The men struggled with the coffin. Lakhan complained that the ice made the coffin too heavy to carry and too cold to grip. One of the men rebuked him and they continued to struggle with it, inching towards the stairs.

The crowd grew outside the cottage. Soon, the whole of New Dam would be here. They were entering the yard and bottomhouse, forming a queue behind the coffin as it was carried upstairs. Women began to wail at the sight of the coffin. Mariam's father, who had been sitting in the shade of the tamarind tree near the public road, was being helped back to his cottage. The crowd cleared a path for him. People touched him sympathetically. June found herself trapped in the middle of the queue on the stairs, then swept indoors eventually. The crowd barely held from crowding round the coffin. The driver became flustered and shouted at people to keep back. He waved his arms in the air. June held on to the window sill and watched as the coffin was opened.

The driver gave instructions for the trestles, wooden planks, rags and aluminium basins in the hearse to be brought up. His instructions were relayed back to the roadside, then the equipment was passed along the crowd, up the stairs and into the cottage.

The trestles and planks were arranged into a table, then the lid and sides of the coffin were removed. Nani prayed more intensely in Hindi. The crowd was silenced by the sight of Mariam's corpse encased in ice. Jack and Lakhan, Mariam's brothers, were drunk. They came forward, the smell of rum strong on them. Jack was quiet but Lakhan began to groan with grief.

June did not feel the fear she expected to feel. It was too much like a dream. Mariam was wearing a frilly white night-gown. Someone had combed out her hair so it lay like a pillow under her, and her face was more peaceful and happy than her most friendly expression ever seemed in life. She looked asleep, not dead. In life, she was always busy, always brisk. She never looked as at peace as she looked now.

They lifted the entire block of ice and rested it on the table, then placed the basins under it to catch the drops. The driver instructed Nani to have the women in to prepare the corpse for burial soon, the ice would melt quickly. Nani sent messengers to fetch the women from Pheasant, including Miss K, who knew how to prepare bodies for burial.

Boysie arrived in the cottage. He spent a few minutes looking at the corpse then he turned and left the cottage again. When he appeared on the landing, men began to shout angrily in the yard. Lakhan's voice was loudest. There was wild talk among the younger men about revenge. June went to sit with the women and children under the house. The path and yard were crowded – they stretched to the public road.

Lakhan sat with Boysie and the men in the yard. He was still hysterical from seeing Mariam's corpse. He wept continuously and drank. He became loud again, screaming abuse and revenge. Boysie and his men dragged him to a corner of the yard and washed his face to try and calm him. Lakhan began to fight with them. When he could not get at them with his fists he began to rip off the paling staves and swing wildly at the crowd nearby. Then he broke through the crowd and ran upstairs where he terrorised the women there. He cursed them, saying they were not Madrasi, that they hated Madrasi people, especially their funerals, let them all go away and leave him to bury his sister with a Madrasi funeral. The women fled the cottage and Lakhan stood on the landing and shouted out more of his rage, brandishing the paling stave. Some of his friends joined him on the landing. They passed rum around. When they were tired of this they left the landing and went downstairs to the kitchen. The women returned to the cottage and locked the doors. Lakhan and his friends cooked, ate, then left the yard and headed for the canefields.

Boysie was soon called up to the cottage by Nani Dharamdai. She demanded to know what would happen when the coffin was brought out; was Mariam going to have a good funeral, with the proper ritual being done, or was it all for politics? She made him promise that the procession would stop five times on the way to the burial ground. Boysie promised that the rituals would be observed. She criticised him for stirring up so much politics around the funeral. Boysie said it was not his fault, it was the overseers, the soldiers, the police, the newspapers and radio. He told her she had no understanding of politics at all, she was one of those people who liked to believe that men like him created politics. He said politics existed all the time. He said Mariam had understood that. Nani did not believe that Boysie had any influence, that he could keep order; she would say the mantras now, before the procession. Boysie became irritated with her and told her to do as she liked. He marched downstairs. A little later, she could be heard reciting the mantras in the cottage.

The longer the crowd waited for the procession, the more their memories of Mariam were stirred, especially the memory of her killing and the imprisonment of Ralph which followed. There was more wild talk among the younger men about revenge – they would storm the police station and free Ralph, they would burn the canefields in all the villages and finish the plantation once and for all, they would sooner die like Mariam than live like slaves. Boysie cautioned them to keep their heads, there were reporters in the crowd. He pointed to the public road: there were all kinds of people there, they had come from New Amsterdam, Corentyne and all the villages in Canefields, let them see that New Dam people could behave with pride.

At four o'clock the drummers and dancers arrived to lead the procession. Lakhan and Jack returned with their friends from the canefields and selected the coffin-bearers. The women emerged from the cottage and joined the women under the bottomhouse. Boysie and Lakhan led the bearers upstairs and soon they emerged with the coffin on their shoulders. The crowd stirred and pressed forward. At the bottom of the stairs the lid of the coffin was removed and people began to pass along for a last look at Mariam. June was taken round the coffin twice by the crushing, encircling crowd.

The image of Mariam encased in ice was replaced now by the image of her lying like a bride in an expensive coffin with a white silky interior. Her skin looked fresh from the ice. They had dried her well, put make-up on her face, put on her jewellery, and dressed her in a long white dress which covered her toes. Flowers were sprinkled over her. Her face was happy and peaceful, as if she were asleep still. The gold of the jewellery reflected the sun. She looked like a waiting bride.

June left the yard for the path and found Lucille and Cyrus among the crowd which was sheltering under the tamarind tree. Lucille scolded her for various things, not having her lunch, her bath, coming here without permission; the sooner the ban on movement outside the village was lifted the better, she could go back to school.

Cyrus calmed her. 'Lucille, not now, this is not the time or place.'

To Lucille, this was all hysteria, a sign that these people could not control their lives. Standing with Lucille, June felt

144

she could hear her thoughts. To Lucille, it was Mariam's fate, which she had chosen. It was all their fault for being slaves, they brought disaster on themselves, she had no sympathy at all for them. She felt how sure Lucille was about her attitudes to New Dam. Although she was here at the funeral, she was aloof from it. She did not feel what Nani felt, or what Boysie felt. She was only here for manners' sake.

14 FREEDOM TALKS

The funeral procession moved away from the path with Lakhan, Jack and their father, Dookhie, at its head. Lakhan was still drunk with rum and hysteria. He danced wildly, possessed, inspiring the other dancers. The paths and public road were too narrow for the crowd. They swelled across the road onto the parapets and into front yards. The crush was so great they were unable to stop the five times Nani had asked. She had performed the Hindu rites of cremation but it was into a grave that Mariam would go, her body prepared according to Miss K's African customs. Their rituals, from birth to death, had to be abandoned or adapted. Nani's voice was a voice from the past which the present shoved aside. As the procession tailed away along the public road, she stood on the landing with her *lota* in her hand, praying in Hindi.

There were men in the crowd who had pleaded for observance of the rites, asking Boysie to stop now, and four more times before they reached the grave, but their voices were drowned by conflicting voices shouting abuse and revenge against the governor and politicians in Georgetown. Their anger drove the procession forward, hurried Mariam's passage to the grave. The procession climbed the southern high bridge then turned to follow the canal before turning south again. When the tail of the procession reached the bridge, the noise faded and the dust they had stirred up in their wake began to settle. Only the women remained at Mariam's cottage, in the yard, bottomhouse, and on the path outside.

June and her parents left the path for the public road. Lucille began to complain about the disorderliness and hysteria of the funeral. 'Nani tried her best but they wouldn't listen to her. They are barbarians.'

146

The outside visitors were still standing along the public road. They were the people from beyond the neighbouring villages, people whose relatives worked on the plantations, who came this way to go to church or attend weddings or funerals. This funeral had brought them out in larger numbers than usual. It had brought out the junior staff too, and the local overseers, who exchanged greetings with Cyrus. The fishing community from Sheet Anchor were here, as well as carpenters, mechanics, tailors, taxi-drivers, road-workers, servants, market vendors. There were people who worked in jobs which took them beyond their homes – teachers, sailors, porters, the tinsmith and jeweller. Some of these people were loud in their criticism of the rowdy politics, the drinking and abusive language at the funeral. They said it was not a proper funeral, there should be another one, a real funeral, that Mariam's spirit would not rest because of the rowdy burial she was given. They shook their heads and said it would bring bad luck. Others of the crowd argued that it was right for people to be angry otherwise the governor and the overseers, and the politicians in Georgetown would think they could do anything they liked; that those who criticised the funeral were jealous that New Dam was at the centre of a national drama – the shooting had been reported on the radio and in the newspapers, even broadcast on the B.B.C World Service.

Merle Searwar and her parents had come to the funeral. They were standing with Louise Sampson and her parents. Lucille and Cyrus greeted the Sampsons who introduced them to the Searwars.

Joseph Searwar offered his handshake to Cyrus and Lucille. 'Hello, I am very pleased to meet you.' He patted June on the head. 'And you, young lady, I hear you don't want to come back to school. You have missed a few days' lessons. You don't like us, you don't like New Amsterdam.'

Lucille apologised, 'It was all the disturbances she saw. She has had a lot of bad experiences, seeing the shooting and so on. Nurse said she should stay home a little.'

Searwar counselled Lucille. 'The longer you keep her at home, the more she will want to return to school.' He lifted a finger at June. 'You will have to go back to school you know.'

'No,' June said rudely. She did not like him taking authority over her, and making her look stupid. Even Louise's parents were looking at her with disapproval. She wondered why they were still standing here trying to feel important; they were supposed to be mourning Mariam. 'I don't want to go to school!'

'You see?' Lucille exclaimed. 'She is a stubborn child. She wants to have her own way.'

They were all standing in the middle of the road, in the hot sun, in their best clothes. They were not going to leave until they had done or said something to make them feel as important as they looked.

Mr. Searwar continued to pick on her. 'You are really upsetting your parents you know.' He was giving her a strange look. He asked her, 'What would make you go back to school?'

Her mother answered for her. 'As I told Anna, if all her primary school friends were going there too. She has a bee in her bonnet about being the only child from New Dam having to go to New Amsterdam High School. And now that the Brijlall boy is in jail makes it worse!'

Searwar said, 'Yes, I've heard that the Brijlall boy is her friend. Friends for a long time?'

Lucille answered, 'Yes.'

'I know he is innocent. We are fighting to get him released. The new lawyers' association in New Amsterdam is studying his case carefully. We have some young lawyers who are not afraid to question some of the estate's practices. I told the governor I am no supporter of the communists, but justice is justice. Mariam Motoo was killed unlawfully. That boy is imprisoned unlawfully. The Governor, the estate management, must accept it or else they are giving more cause to the communists, giving them martyrs to their cause. I want to see this country free, not involved in the cold war. I am a Guianese, not British like some people say they are, but Guianese.'

Now Lucille spoke directly to Mrs. Searwar. 'I wish you could use your good influence to get June to go back to school.'

Mrs. Searwar nodded and said to June, 'I am sure June will do the right thing in the end if we don't press her too much. Sometimes that is all children want.'

Mistress Sampson said, 'June you are hurting your parents, but you are hurting yourself most of all, my dear.'

June complained bitterly. 'I don't want no education.'

Lucille apologised again. 'Ever since she saw the shooting she does not bother to show any respect at all.'

Mistress Sampson declared, 'Without an education you will be useless to your country. Don't you want to be useful?'

'No,' June declared.

Joseph Searwar said, 'June, let me and you strike up a bargain. I will get Ralph out of jail if you promise me in exchange that you will go back to school!'

June was sure that Joseph Searwar was only playing but at the back of her mind stirred the suspicion that he might have it in his power to get Ralph out of jail. She said nothing but he smiled as if he had read her mind and knew he had planted the doubt which would lead her back to school.

His wife chided him. 'Joseph, don't raise the child's hopes.'

Cyrus put on his hat, a sign that he wanted to leave. He took June's hand and said, 'Excuse us,' to the group.

Mr. Searwar detained them. 'June, give me an answer.'

She was sure he was joking, making fun. She looked up at her father who returned her look and smiled as if he was telling her it was only a joke, not serious, local people had no such power.

Mr. Searwar spoke to Mr. Sampson, 'Arthur, will you tell Mr. Lehall here? Back me up? Tell him, I am not one of those businessmen who only make money for their own sake?' He turned to Cyrus. 'I like to put the money I make, and my children's skills, back into this country. All my children are doing things which are useful to this country.' He counted on his fingers: 'Teaching, medicine, law, engineering.' He looked at June, 'I am interested, really interested, in your education.' He smiled. 'But you don't believe me. You don't believe that your own people, that Guianese men and women, can have real power and influence over their lives.' He turned around

149

and spoke to the women. 'That is what we are up against, ladies.' He shook his head. 'It is terrible that we are not free yet. You see how I speak to the child and she doesn't believe me? Our children are growing up today and still feeling their parents are slaves.'

His wife interrupted him. 'Joseph, you are boring the child. Come let us go home and leave the people to mourn their dead. There has been too much excitement.'

He countered, 'Just a minute, just a minute.' He placed his hand on June's shoulder. 'Jail is no place for Ralph, and staying out of school is no place for you either. You both belong in your respective places. For that reason we will get Ralph out of jail and I am sure that, in return, you will go back to school. You will?'

June felt sure he was behaving like this because he wanted to be known and remembered in New Dam where this historic thing had happened, so historic, it was in the Georgetown, British and American newspapers, and on the B.B.C. World Service. Yet she was so desperate for Ralph's freedom, she found herself searching her mind for an answer to give to Mr. Searwar, even if he was not serious, even though, up to now, he had nothing to do with Ralph, and nothing to do with New Dam.

Cyrus spoke quietly, 'She will go to school.' There was a coldness in his voice; he did not like the interference. In the end, he always went back to Boysie's position. Then he ended the exchanges by saying he had to go to work.

The men raised their hats to the women and they parted company. Lucille began to fret as soon as they were on their way: why had Cyrus said June would go back to school, he did not mean it, he had done nothing to force her back, nothing at all.

Cyrus snapped, 'But you think he mean it?'

'Of course he means it, he has power.'

'He is just a capitalist.'

'You sound just like Boysie!'

'And you surprised?'

They walked along with the tension strong and silent between them.

The next day, Saturday, Overseers Sampson and Beardsley came to visit them. June was helping Lucille in the garden. Cyrus was working on a car in Mr. Easen's yard.

First, the overseers held a discussion in the yard with Cyrus, then they all went upstairs. Now she knew why Lucille had been cleaning the cottage from early that morning. In the cottage they sat around the kitchen table and Lucille brought them glasses of iced sorrel.

Overseer Beardsley began to question June. 'How long have you known Ralph Brijlall?'

'Since St. Peter's school.'

Lucille added, 'From the preparatory class.'

Overseer Sampson was writing everything down, in a small, blue hardcover notebook, the kind used by the foreman when he came to the village to write up shift notices on the blackboard which was nailed to one of the lantern posts.

Overseer Beardsley asked, 'He was a good friend? No problems at all with him?'

June answered quickly, before Lucille could answer for her. 'No! No problems. Ralph used to stop the fighting at school.'

Cyrus agreed. 'It is true. Ralph was a good boy, boisterous like any normal child.'

'I have to ask you these specific questions. Did he ever steal?'

'No.'

'Did he ever threaten anyone?'

'No.'

'Had he ever spoken about setting fire to the canefields or overseers' houses? The Government in Georgetown is taking all this very seriously.'

'No.'

Overseer Beardsley paused before he asked the next question. 'Did you ever see him strike or injure anyone recently?'

'No.'

Overseer Beardsley turned to Overseer Sampson. 'I think that is all we need. This will help us to get him out of jail.'

This surprised June – she was sure they had come here to look for reasons to keep Ralph in jail. They had not been able to pin the blame for the fires on anyone. They had only the security guard's evidence that Ralph had stoned Sarah Beardsley. Only he had been seen committing a violent action although everyone on strike had a motive for setting fire to the overseer's house. No one had said anything about Overseer Johnson and Sookdeo's girlfriend – that was the hidden motive which the whole village and Overseer Johnson himself were keeping quiet. In New Dam, they knew that overseers were not punished for molesting women, but they were surprised Overseer Johnson had said nothing. They had expected him to point the finger at Sookdeo. The fact that he did not puzzled them at first, and the longer his silence lasted, the more the impression was growing that perhaps the overseers were in a less strong position than they used to be. While they all wondered and waited, Ralph stayed in jail. Sookdeo had been badly wounded and was still in hospital, but he would be all right eventually. They were going to charge him with assault, but that was a drama still to come. All the attention which they had attracted had gone to their heads and they swarmed round the P.P.P. and G.A.W.U. representatives when they came to the villages in Canefields, though Boysie, Mr. Easen, Cyrus, and many of the older men stayed away from them. It was the younger men who flocked to meetings with these representatives; they promised to make it a nationwide issue in the elections, and this promised to prolong the excitement which had to do with feeling part of the outside world at last. All the time, Ralph's chances of getting out of jail did not improve; they seemed to forget all about him. Each minute he was in jail seemed like a year to June.

'Would you like to visit Ralph?' Overseer Beardsley asked June.

Lucille asked, 'In the jail?'

June answered, 'Yes.'

He turned to Cyrus. 'Cyrus? You agree to it?'

Cyrus answered. 'Yes, yes.' He said to Lucille, 'Is only the police station in Good Land, not the New Amsterdam jail. There is only one cell at Good Land station.' He asked the overseers to wait while he spoke with June. He took her aside, telling her that she should not say anything at all that would give them cause to keep Ralph in prison.

Lucille reproached him. 'Overseer Beardsley is only trying to help Ralph.'

'No, there is a lot of politics going on,' Cyrus insisted. 'Everyone looking for credit here. You have to be very careful with everything you say and do. The country going through a very difficult time. The place full of propaganda and nothing to show for it, just a lot of excitement and people all wanting the credit for releasing Ralph.'

Lucille still disagreed. 'Not Overseer Beardsley. He is going against the other foreign overseers. He always goes against them.'

'In the end he is an overseer, when push comes to shove.'

They returned to the landing where the overseers were waiting and Overseer Beardsley told June they would call for Sarah on the way. He did not explain why he was taking Sarah too, and it made her hesitate, but her desire to see Ralph was stronger than her suspicions, so she got into the overseer's jeep, they in the front, she standing at the back, holding on to the rail. She seemed to have been everywhere these last few weeks but she had never thought she would be driving through the estate in an overseer's jeep.

Overseer Sampson parted company with them at Overseer Beardsley's gate. There was a new security guard at the gate and he telephoned for Sarah. She came cycling along the path, dropped her bicycle inside the gate and came running towards the jeep, as eager as ever for play. The jeep turned around and they drove towards the forest, past New Dam, past Reliance, Adelphi and Betsy Ground where the smell of the river began and the flat wasteland on the left side of the road contrasted with the tall trees on the right.

At Good Land, the police station and post office occupied the same large compound, with the courthouse standing in a compound of its own. These buildings were painted in official colonial colours, cream and maroon, and a British flag flew from the roof of the courthouse. All the official buildings and public places in New Amsterdam were painted in these colours too, and the older villages in Canefields had used these colours, when they could afford to paint their cottages, but for many years the overseers' quarters had used different colours, green for the roofs and white for the boards and pillars, and new villages like New Dam copied these colours and marked themselves out as belonging to a different era.

All during the drive she and Sarah said nothing to each other. June was afraid to speak in case Sarah talked about the stoning, but the English girl was enjoying her own freedom so much her mind did not seem to be on that at all; she was looking all around her greedily, feeding her eyes on the scenes which passed by. They had passed a house being moved on a truck. It excited Sarah and she begged her father to stop. They passed a house where a large group of beggars were being fed in the front yard; they were sitting on the grass with huge banana leaves spread before them and a whole family was queuing, each with a large bowl or basin or pot of food, to ladle out portions of curry, dhal, rice and roti as the beggars ate from the leaves. There were children swimming in the canals; the shops were packed with Saturday shoppers and the roadside vendors were selling their best crops of vegetables, provisions and fruits. Carpenters were at work on a new house, helped by a swarm of small boys. Women stood on their landings and fanned rice in the breeze, throwing the grains high from the sifters and scattering the dust and shells into the breeze, catching the grains as they fell in a straight line back into the sifters – a skill girls learnt early. Bottomhouses were being daubed, water fetched from standpipes, drains were being cleaned, parapets weeded, gardens tended, babies breastfed in hammocks; cricket was being played on the paths and any spare patch of ground. Between the tall trees where boats were kept, a barrel of tar was being boiled in preparation for tarring a new boat. June saw how hungrily Sarah took in all these scenes and guessed it was a regular treat which her father gave her, driving through the villages on the busiest day of the week. There were no tall fences here, no huge lawns and enclosed verandahs – there was no privacy at all; you could see everybody's business, even courting couples or the legs and arms of someone bathing in a wooden closet in a yard. At the rice mill, the women were treading the padi, walking in long queues up and down the asphalted ground, the grain thick to their ankles. At the saw mill, rough, thick planks of wood were being loaded on the trucks. While Sarah was enjoying her freedom, Ralph was locked away from all this.

Overseer Beardsley, told them to wait in the jeep while he went to the station to speak to Sergeant Richards first. When he was gone, Sarah began to talk. She said that they were all going away to England, the whole family, to live in Sussex where her parents were born. Annie had already gone and they had spoken to her on the telephone; she sounded happy. Her father did not really want to go, he said he preferred his life here, but he had decided it was best for the whole family. Sarah said nothing about Ralph.

Overseer Beardsley returned to the jeep, and told June to come with him into the station. He told Sarah to wait where she was.

In the station, Sergeant Richards stood behind a wooden counter, a large notebook in front of him. He pointed to the book and showed June where she should sign. He explained that all visitors to the station had to sign this book. She did not feel afraid of him although she had expected to. He looked very different without his riot helmet, ammunition belt, rifle and boots. On the public road, on the day of the shooting, he had been aggressive and threatening, now he looked like a sleepy, bald-pated man at home in the tiny wooden station. When he moved from behind the counter she saw that he was barefoot and was wearing the minimum uniform, only a short-sleeved open-necked shirt and blue trousers. He wore no badge, no stripes, brass buttons or gunbelt. It did not seem this was really a jail. There was a smell of cooking, he would be having his lunch soon with his family, who probably lived with him upstairs. There was something small and safe about the place, so unlike all the excitement of the last few days. Her anxieties for Ralph began to subside. Perhaps her father and Mr. Easen were right, that if Georgetown politicians left them

155

alone they could run their own lives in peace. But Boysie said the peace was not real, that it covered up the fact that they were still slaves on the estate, that they had to fight against it. But look what happened when they did – disaster, panic, confusion, killing, hatred rocking their existence like an earthquake, rocking their ground so hard it would break, destroy the little bit of neighbourliness they did have, that they managed to scrape out of their plantation existence. Cyrus often said it was better to have this, a little bit of neighbourliness, than to have nothing at all. He was more afraid of having nothing at all, more afraid than Boysie, who was more reckless and would back down only when destruction stared him in the face, back down because he could see his community under threat. If the Georgetown politicians took over their fight, would they know when to back down for the sake of communities they did not live in, or would they fight even if it meant communities had to perish?

Sergeant Richards led her down a short, narrow corridor to a small wooden room where Ralph sat on an iron-framed bed, a bare coconut-matting mattress folded on one side of it. He looked thin and weary. Sergeant Richards left them, not closing the door behind him.

She joked with Ralph, 'You getting plenty rest in jail!'

He smiled half-heartedly and pulled his face. 'You come and you 'in bring nothing, some nice fowl? Sergeant wife only cookin' cook-up rice and all kind tomato stew. She can' cook nothing else.'

They laughed, then the silence fell again. The floor was dusty. 'I will bring something next time.'

'Is awright, man. My mother does bring plenty food. I only talkin'.'

'Mariam get buried.'

'Police kill she,' he declared bitterly, 'and put me in jail as if I do it.'

'They can't keep you in jail. They don't have evidence you burn any house. You only pelt the girl; they don't lock anybody up for that.'

This did not impress Ralph. The fact was, he was in jail and

156

Sergeant Richards was not letting him out. They could hear the voices of the two men in the next room.

She said, 'People trying hard to get you out of jail.'

He sneered. 'Who?'

'Overseer Beardsley, and the merchant from New Amsterdam, Joseph Searwar...'

'Since when merchant care about we? Nowadays politician from town want we vote. Now merchant want something?'

'Joseph Searwar say a young lawyer in New Amsterdam studying your case and will look after you for free.'

He shook his head. 'I don' trus' them. Tell them don' worry. I will tell Ma, tell them don't worry.'

'My father say is the politics. Everybody looking for credit, but you not concerned with that, you only concerned with getting out. You must let them get you out.'

He flung his arms wide. 'I will stay right he'. Let we people strike and strike and strike and burn down everything. Let it be the last plantation.'

She became angry with him. 'Stupidy, you really stupid. You is the one in jail. You is the one they catch. You will pay for it.'

'They can't do me nothing.

'They can keep you here till you old and dead,' she said ruthlessly.

'It better than estate work. I does get food here. I don' have to do nothing but eat and sleep and rest.'

'They can't keep you here. They will send you to jail in town then you will meet some real criminals, murderers.'

He sucked his teeth, uncaring. 'Boysie will get me out.'

'Boysie can't get you out. He refusing to talk to anybody. Only people like Overseer Beardsley and Joseph Searwar can influence the sergeant. Boysie has no influence at all over him. Boysie just insulting him every time they talk. Sergeant Richards might just be keeping you here to spite Boysie. Nowadays you don't know why people do a thing. Sometimes people just want to spite mati. Plenty spite politics around now.'

'Why you bad-talkin' Boysie?'

'Truth not bad-talk. Listen, you should talk about Sookdeo

157

and what Overseer Johnson do. Nobody bring that one up yet, and that is the reason why everything, all the trouble, start, never mind the politics. People private story an' politics all getting mixed up nowadays.'

'You mad? You want them kill Sookdeo? Then he will get the blame, he will get jail.'

She shook her head. 'No. Tell Overseer Beardsley. He is the man to tell, nobody else, and he will make sure Sookdeo don't get punish.'

He shook his head. 'You don't know overseer. They never stop overseer molesting women.'

'Overseer Beardsley looking for a reason to get you out. He going back to England and perhaps he want to do one last good thing.'

'How you know? He tell you so?' he challenged her.

'He come to question me this morning and I had a feeling he know that I see you pelt his daughter but he din' press me to tell the truth. I tell him I din' see you do it. He want you to get off. Overseers can still do what they like. Normally is Boysie or Mr. Easen or my father who can settle New Dam problems but this one get too big for them. This is Overseer Beardsley chance to help us. Overseer Beardsley going away. Tell him, Ralph, and get out of jail before things get worse; you have people who want it to get worse, who don't care about you.'

He would not respond and she became angry with him and told him he was ignorant. Still he did not respond.

After a few minutes he said, 'One thing you don't understand is Sergeant Richards. He working for outside people now, people outside New Dam who never used to want anything to do with New Dam before.'

'But outside people don't have power yet in Canefields, so is the overseer he still got to listen to. If you leave it too long, outside politics will take hold and then the sergeant would have to listen to that. But right now, Overseer Beardsley there with him. You going to talk to him?'

He shrugged and she went outside, only to find the office empty and the overseer and the sergeant standing in the

158

compound with Boysie and a group of men approaching them from the gate. She stood in the doorway and waited to see what would happen next. Sarah Beardsley was still there, in the jeep, on the far side of the compound, separated from her father by Boysie and his men.

Richards hurried back into the station and reappeared wearing his boots, stripes, badge and hat. He was still fastening his belt when Boysie stopped a few yards in front of him and declared that he had heard that the overseer was here and demanded to know what he wanted with Ralph.

'Go 'long you way, Boysie,' Sergeant Richards said contemptuously, 'Go 'long.'

Boysie stood his ground. He was not going anywhere. His face was full of distrust. His men also stood their ground, defiant.

Sergeant Richards asked. 'You all intend to stand up there whole day?'

'We can stand up here as long as we like. This is public property. We 'in trespassing. You all 'in takin' Ralph to jail in town.'

The overseer reasoned with Boysie, 'Ralph is staying here.'

Boysie avoided the overseer's eyes. He could hardly bear to have any contact at all with him. He complained bitterly to the sergeant, complaints he wanted the overseer to overhear. 'Overseer don't have no right to come in our village. What he want?'

The sergeant said, 'If you want talk to the overseer, you should lead a delegation to the factory, don't come to my station to do it.' He laughed loudly. He was enjoying his power over Boysie.

Overseer Beardsley explained that he was not here on any kind of business which would harm Ralph, he had only brought Cyrus' daughter to visit Ralph.

One of Boysie's men sniggered. 'He talkin' lie man. They want carry Ralph to New Amsterdam jail, then Georgetown jail. Georgetown politicians want humble we, show we they got power over we. They want use Ralph to set example.'

The overseer insisted. 'Please be rational. I have been

159

pleading Ralph's case with the sergeant, asking him to let us settle this among ourselves, without bringing in politicians and lawyers from outside. It will become too big for us to handle, and it is Ralph who will suffer.'

Another of Boysie's men declared, 'Is all one and the same – overseer, police, lawyer, politician. All against we.'

The overseer begged them to listen to him. He said that he knew that the only reason Ralph was being held was because he had stoned his daughter, but he had told the sergeant he wanted to withdraw the charge. There was no longer a reason for holding Ralph. He suggested they should go home and leave him to settle the whole matter with the sergeant. A confrontation now would lead from one thing to another.

The more the overseer spoke, the more agitated Boysie became. He could not bear to take advice from the overseer now, when all his life they had given him orders. He ignored the overseer and addressed the sergeant again, 'Look here, Richards, I telling you, village affairs is for village people to settle.'

Sergeant Richards ignored Boysie. He waited for Boysie or the overseer to make the next move.

The overseer sighed, gave a loose salute and stepped back. 'Well gentlemen, I will take my leave of you now. Good day to you all.' He went to the jeep; started the motor and turned it round to face the men. They did not part to make way for him. The jeep's exhaust trembled and stirred the dust from under the wheels.

The public road was asphalted here. There was a string of full punts of cane on the canal to the north of the station. There was a hardware shop across the road, a group of men in the doorway watching the scene. In the small settlement behind the shop, people were about in their yards. Some small boys were racing skeleton bicycle wheels, testing their skill at racing them, with only a stick to balance and speed them along the rough paths.

The longer the men blocked his way, the more the overseer's calmness faded. Boysie and his men were letting him feel the full weight of their hostility. Sergeant Richards could see

160

that the overseer was under pressure and was doing nothing at all to help him, he was not moved at all by this confrontation, he had no interest in it. Sarah began to cry, quietly first, then louder, like a baby. Overseer Beardsley hugged her.

June turned to see Ralph near her, watching the scene. He had seen and heard everything.

15 THE LAST ENGLISH PLANTATION

Now there was a commotion on the public road. A man was climbing up the main telegraph pole outside the post office. He climbed as if he were climbing a coconut tree and men stood below, urging him on. He was attracting crowds from Good Land Settlement and cyclists were stopping to watch. A donkey cart cantered past; the driver would take the news along all the villages and people would come to join in. Now the Postmaster came running out of the post office, shaking his fist at the man on the pole and shouting abuse at him. When the man reached the top of the post he drew a cutlass from his belt and chopped at the wire until it fell loose like a piece of string, then the man shouted, 'Now Richards can't telephone soldier to come and shoot we.'

The Postmaster came striding into the compound. 'Sergeant, what are you going to do about that? These people are damaging government property, man! They can't do that! You are the law of the government here!'

The sergeant spoke calmly. 'Is awright Postmaster. You go back to the post office. I will handle this.'

The postmaster looked round him angrily and went striding back across the compound to the post office. The man who had cut the wire was on the ground now, retrieving his cutlass from the grass. He walked away towards Good Land Settlement. Sergeant Richards walked straight up to the crowd and folded his arms.

'You all going home?' He demanded. The crowd was silent; more men and women were joining them. There was a steady trickle coming into the settlement from the north and south. He pointed to Overseer Beardsley and his daughter.

'Well, this gentleman wants to go home, so clear the way and let him through.'

No one obeyed. Mitch's taxi appeared on the bridge. Cyrus was sitting beside him in the front seat and Mr. Easen was in the back. Mitch hooted the horn and swore at the crowd. When they would not move he wanted to know whether they were sitting on their ears or what. He let out Cyrus and Mr. Easen, then drove away towards Pheasant. Cyrus and Mr. Easen joined Boysie at the front of the crowd.

'Good day, Sergeant,' Mr. Easen greeted, touching his forehead in mock salute. He began to explain to Sergeant Richards that he had just remembered that there was an act passed in 1946, ten years ago, which prevented the plantation from using child labour. Legally, Ralph was not an employee of the plantation, nor a member of any union, he was an ordinary child of the state, under the state's protection, which meant the sergeant's protection, but more important, he was the community's responsibility, especially his mother's, who had been sent for and would soon be here; she was the person Ralph should rightfully be with right now.

There were different reactions to this among the crowd. Someone laughed and asked Mr. Easen if he kept his brains in mothballs, it had taken him so long to remember an act passed in 1946. Another said the overseers knew, and they knew, that children under age should not be employed, but people were desperate for money and the overseers didn't care. Others said the laws passed in this country were passed for businessmen and civil servants in Georgetown, not for country people. But one man shouted that they should prosecute the overseers, as if he had not heard the comment about the law being on the side of Georgetown. Resentment welled up in the crowd and the men began to swear idly among themselves, spelling out, reciting and rehearsing their grievances.

Into this confusion in the compound rode Lavender Jones and her father. He was towing her on his carrier bicycle, with all his tools strung around the handlebars and strips of guttering tied to the handle. He was a cheerful man, and he laughed

163

to see the confrontation between the sergeant and the crowd. He declared that he had come to fix the gutters and that was what he was going to do; he worked in all weathers and circumstances, they could go on killing each other. He took his ladder to the back of the station and could be heard whistling as he began to work. Lavender came to stand with June and Ralph; she told June she was now working at the police station, doing housework for the sergeant's family, until they could find another school for her to go to – if not, Rachael and Mr. Sam would coach her at home.

The sergeant had thought hard about a reply to Mr. Easen's challenge and now he spoke to him, 'Easen, you think we in Canefields are a law unto ourselves?'

Mr. Easen declared, 'I never said so. With great respect I never said so.'

Cyrus spoke, 'Sergeant you know we solve our problems without going to law.'

'You saying the law is useless?' the sergeant demanded.

Mr. Easen intervened. 'Far from it. We are law-abiding citizens, the most law-abiding you will find anywhere.'

Boysie grumbled. 'Easen, this 'in nothing to do with you at all. But if you right, Ralph must come out'a jail right now.'

Cyrus cautioned Boysie to proceed slowly, to talk, not fight his way through this situation. He told Boysie he was like a bull in a china shop – one of Lucille's expressions.

But the sergeant wanted to take up Boysie. 'Must? Must? Who say anything *must* happen? I am the law here.'

Mr. Easen lectured the sergeant. 'No man is a law unto himself. We are a community and that is where you have to have agreement before the law can come into effect.'

The sergeant laughed very hard at this and asked Mr. Easen which age, and which country he thought he was living in; he had lived too long, his brain was not working at all. 'Let me tell you,' the sergeant said, pointing north, 'That is where the law is made, Georgetown, by the leaders of this country.'

The whole crowd was united against this idea, all the differences, racial, cultural, work – forgotten. The idea that they were ruled by laws which were discussed and made in Georgetown was unacceptable. It threw them partly into confusion, partly into rage at Georgetown. Sergeant Richards laughed, nodding his head, and declared, 'You all think you is lord and master here? You 'in lord and master here!'

Someone at the back of the crowd shouted angrily. 'Neither you, Richards. You 'in lord and master neither!'

All this time, Overseer Beardsley's jeep was running, waiting to leave while they argued among themselves.

Their old packed earth road was going to be replaced by a new road after the next elections – this had been promised them. The Jagans and Burnhams of this world were invading their lives, once isolated and impenetrable. They said Jagan was a country boy once, a sugar estate lad, but he had gone abroad and learnt his politics from books, while they had grown into big men on the estate and learnt their politics the hard way. As for Burnham, he was completely a book-trained man, they said he talked like an Englishman. All these arguments went back and forth between them while Overseer Beardsley was waiting to leave the compound, leave the country.

In the meantime Sergeant Richards had been learning his own politics, right there in New Dam. A few days ago he had put on a riot helmet and worn an ammunition belt and carried a gun in opposition to them for the first time in his life. He had seen what an army, guns, a police force could do, how, in the end, whether or not the laws were made in Georgetown, whether or not communities held together in the different villages of Guiana, the gun, the military could wield the greatest influence. In Sergeant Richards, Mr. Easen had a new enemy, and he glared at him with a mixture of helplessness and rage as he heard his contempt for the law of community.

Overseer Beardsley became impatient, seeing that they had forgotten him, and honked the horn and pressed the accelerator. They cleared a path and he drove away, out of the police compound, onto the public road, and was safely on his way home. June watched Sarah turning round to prolong her last glimpse of the people of Canefields.

165

Mr. Easen continued to glare at Sergeant Richards and the sergeant returned the stare barefacedly. 'Who the hell you think you are, Richards? Your job is to keep law here in Canefields, not in Georgetown. We call you when we need you, which is hardly ever, because we always settle our own disputes. Only when we can't, you come in.'

The sergeant sucked his teeth. 'Times changing, Easen. You go back to slave days where you belong. Black man 'in slave in this country no more. You can continue living like slave with coolie 'pon sugar plantation. You don' know black man lef plantation long time now? You still living in ancient history? Well, road getting build now. You can ride 'pon you bicycle on smooth smooth road all the way to Georgetown now and feel like if you lying down 'pon Dunlopillo bed now, man. Take the road to freedom at last, Easen. You is leftover slave man, hangin' 'bout with coolie still. I come from West Coast, I know better. Look, first time I come live he' I get a shock fo' see bush nigger, people who never see civilisation since they come from Africa to this country, backward people who does make people think all African backward, still living in the forest. Well, that's what you is, Easen, a bush nigger living here in bush with coolie.'

Mr. Easen shook with rage at being spoken to like this, by a man younger than himself. He shook his finger at him. 'You are a disgrace to your uniform. You have no respect for people older than you, with more experience than you. I will report you to the Superintendent of police.'

The sergeant roared with laughter. 'As soon as he get you letter he will laugh. You are illiterate, you can hardly spell! You all not accustom to meeting you mati coolie and black who can spell, that's why you have no respect for Mr. Burnham.'

Mr. Easen was so shaken by the enormity of the sergeant's contempt, he could think of nothing else to say. Now Boysie stepped forward to confront the sergeant.

Boysie accused him. 'You playing wrong and strong, like Forbes Burnham, creating confusion. Parasite! Is we planta-tion people fight for freedom in this country. Is only we does defy the overseer who hold the real power in this country. The real slaves live in Georgetown where they can't say 'Boo!' to the governor and only bowing and scraping. White people does teach in them schools in Georgetown. Only in country you does see local people teaching. Don' call *we* slave. This is one place you don't find slave. This is the place where slave fight fo' freedom! This is Canje River where they fight and the river run with blood.'

Boysie's speech was not working. It only made the sergeant laugh. Talk of violence and fighting only made the sergeant feel stronger.

Boysie spat on the ground. 'You owe we something, Richards!'

'What I owe you, Boysie?'

'Your blasted freedom!'

This annoyed the sergeant. 'Don' go too far, Boysie.'

'I talking about 1951.'

'What you know about 1951? You all don't even read newspapers. You don't even listen to radio. You don't even leave this place to go anywhere. Bicycle fo' you is the latest scientific invention. What you could tell me about 1951 I don't know, eh?'

'Is a person like we had the ability to go to England and get constitution changed, make sure that all a we, man and woman, cast vote. He had it in he to do it, an you know why? Is because he grow up and see the slavery on plantation, it give he passion to fight fo' freedom. What passion Georgetown people got? Only fo' jealous mati they know. They don' know nothing 'bout revolution!'

The sergeant laughed again. 'Revolution? What you know about revolution, Boysie? This country never had no revolution.'

Boysie pointed his finger at Richards. 'You know blasted well that the PPP under Cheddi Jagan, African, Indian, all races, was united behind him in 1951, and that is how come we get we first legally elected government for the workers in 1953, for the first time in this country. But people hate fo' see poor people win an' from the time it happen all kind people workin'

167

mischief, an' who helpin' most with mischief? Georgetown! Where *you* does get you orders nowadays.'

Now, the tension mounted in the police compound. Boysie was painting a new picture of division, but Sergeant Richards had spoken the truth, they were still too cut off from the outside world to know what to believe. All they could be sure of was that the overseers still ran the sugar plantations. The tension Boysie was planting now, they dissipated with abuse against the plantation system: they began to curse and swear – how they used and abused coolie people, shot and killed them, put children to work, sent people to an early grave, caused sickness, hardship, closed down the hospital, increased workload and decreased pay, no sanitation to talk about, living like pigs and dogs.

Lavender whispered in June's ear: did she know that Sergeant Richards had to keep Ralph in jail or else the police would be blamed for killing Mariam? Her father had told her so. June had believed it was the army that had shot Mariam.

Boysie demanded again that Sergeant Richards release Ralph from jail.

The sergeant said, 'Oh ho, you 'in got use for him in jail no more? Now you know Ralph can't belong to your union he won't be a real martyr if he go to jail, not like Mariam. All this time you never come here to ask me to let him out. You wanted him in jail so that newspapers would keep writing about New Dam.'

Someone in the crowd called the sergeant a black fool. Mr. Easen stepped in quickly, before the sergeant could react. He turned on the man who had said this and asked him why he was showing off his technicality, did he have a degree in Fools to be able to tell the difference between one fool and another? He said it took one fool to know another. Besides, what was the difference between a black fool and a coolie fool, perhaps he could explain that to everyone.

Now Cyrus tried to reason with the sergeant. 'The way I see it, Sergeant, Ralph pelting the child was only a side issue that get dragged into the strike. It had nothing at all to do with it. We all know that really.'

The sergeant backed away a few steps from the crowd while men and women took up Cyrus's idea and grew angrier by the second. They shouted how Ralph was treated with so much injustice; Mr. Easen was right about the 1946 act preventing child labour, Boysie was right about the sugar workers revolution and Cyrus was right that Ralph was being made a scapegoat for the police and army.

Sergeant Richards ran into the station and put on his ammunition belt and gun. He returned to the yard. The flap of his holster was open and the butt of the gun was plain to see on his hip. He raised his arm and signalled that they were to leave the compound. 'Out! Out!' he shouted. 'This is government property and you don't have any peaceful business here to conduct. Get out!'

Mr. Easen reasoned with him. 'All right, Sergeant. You don't have to talk so, don't provoke we.'

'You shut your trap, Easen,' the sergeant ordered, 'And clear out here like the rest of them.'

A brick flew from the back of the crowd and landed against the wall of the station. The sergeant pulled his gun from the holster, pointed it upwards and fired a shot which cracked open the air like lightning. It threw the crowd into uproar and some men and women ran out of the compound, across the road and into the settlement. Those who stayed drew closer into a tight grouping.

Boysie hollered. 'Why the hell you fire gun, eh?'

Mr. Easen turned to face the crowd and advised them to move back to the public road; they should stage their demonstration there, out of the yard; they should not return home, they would all remain here, and keep a vigil as long as they could, taking turns, put pressure on the governor to release Ralph; this way, they would get favourable reports on the B.B.C and local radio and newspapers of the world. If they had a confrontation now with the sergeant, the police and the army (he said they were probably on their way) the whole world would only say they were a ruction people thirsty for violence. They listened to him but waited for Boysie to voice his response. Boysie glared at the sergeant while he made up his mind, then he signalled to the crowd to move back to the public road.

Cyrus signalled to June to join him but before she could, Overseer Beardsley's jeep reappeared on the high bridge. He was honking the horn loudly and Bibi Mahadeo, Ralph's mother, sat beside him in the front seat. Sarah sat in the back seat. He drove through the crowd without slowing down. They were too surprised to block his way although some in the crowd urged it. The jeep reached the sergeant and stopped. The overseer climbed into the back of the jeep and turned to face the crowd.

'Bibi Mahadeo has something to say,' the overseer announced and he helped Bibi to climb over the seat and stand next to him. 'Tell them, Mrs. Mahadeo,' he encouraged.

Bibi was too nervous to speak and the crowd stirred restlessly. One man voiced a suspicion that she had been forced to say something, perhaps bribed to say something, against Ralph. This made her shake her head at the overseer and climb out of the jeep. She went to Cyrus and held his hand. Cyrus asked her what was going on and she began to weep.

The overseer spoke to the crowd. 'Bibi Mahadeo has told us the story behind the burning of Overseer Johnson's house and the fields. You are all right, it had nothing to do with the strike.' He repeated this three times until he had their attention. He continued. 'On my way home when I left you, I met Mrs. Mahadeo on her way here. She was in a very distressed state, afraid that Ralph was going to be taken away to New Amsterdam, and she made a confession to me and asked me to help her.' He told the crowd what Bibi had told him, that Sookdeo had set fire to Overseer Johnson's house in revenge for Overseer Johnson molesting Sookdeo's girlfriend, Yasmin.

The crowd became enraged with the overseer. They declared that if they imprisoned Sookdeo with Ralph there would be trouble. The overseer shook his head and waved his arms for silence.

'Listen to me! Listen to me!' he begged. 'I have not finished. Now listen! I took Mrs. Mahadeo to the manager's house.

There, I asked him to call in the overseers and field managers and we had a conference right there. Overseer Johnson was there.' He turned to Mahadeo and asked her to tell the crowd that this was indeed what had happened. She nodded in agreement and he continued. 'Of course, as you can imagine, there were many there who felt that Sookdeo should be punished very severely. They blamed him for the burning of the canes too. But Bibi Mahadeo insists that Sookdeo did not burn the cane and we have absolutely no proof that he did, or any indication of who did it; it might even have been an accident.' He told them that the conference at the manager's house had agreed after a long discussion, which was very hot-tempered, that Overseer Johnson should return to England and Sookdeo should be pardoned and go free.

The crowd would not believe it. It was not possible. Bibi tried to shout above their voices, that it was true, she had seen and heard the whole discussion. Boysie shouted that they should be silent and listen to Bibi. When they were listening, she backed up Overseer Beardsley's story. It was true she said, although she could not believe it herself, it was exactly what happened. It was the local overseers who put the case against Johnson; they said that the molesting by overseers of women in the fields had to stop and Johnson had to be made an example of.

The overseer turned to the sergeant. 'Sergeant Richards, we have decided the boy must go free now.'

The sergeant refused. 'I have to hear it from the governor in Georgetown.'

'The manager spoke to the governor during our meeting.'

There was silence all around the compound as they took this in. All the excitement of the past few years, the show-downs, and most of all the feeling that working people, in spite of everything, had become a thorn in the side of the British – all this had planted the feeling in them that decisions could no longer be made like this. The British were still here, they had not gone yet.

Overseer Beardsley continued. 'The army is taking orders from the governor. I pressed for them to leave this area. I complained about their presence here and the tension it is causing.'

Boysie shouted. 'And what about the police? You have the power to do anything about the police? And why you don' send away Manager Smith too, eh Beardsley? We don' want no manager who workin' with the blasted governor in Georgetown. You only tryin' to get we back to work!' But there was no conviction in Boysie's voice. He was turning his accusations too rapidly from one enemy to the other: the governor, the manager of the estate, the army, and the local police.

The overseer said. 'I have no interest now whether you go back to work or not. I have resigned from the estate, I am no longer an employee there.'

Boysie pointed his finger at the overseer and yelled, 'You lie!'

The sergeant raised his right hand. He had listened keenly to everything and made his own decision. He asked the crowd to listen to him now, then he shouted to Ralph to come out to the compound. When Ralph appeared, the sergeant beckoned him forward. He told June and Lavender to come forward too and he asked Overseer Beardsley to tell his daughter to leave the jeep and stand with the other children. Sarah Beardsley refused, but her father chided her and demanded that she obey the sergeant. When the children were grouped together he asked them whether they knew each other. They nodded.

'I want you to tell the whole truth and nothing but the truth, you understand?' the sergeant ordered.

There was no response from the children.

Mr. Easen advised, 'Answer the sergeant, come, come.'

Boysie said, 'Ralph, answer yes. Nothing going happen to you. Don' play the fool now. Is awright.'

When Ralph nodded, Lavender, June and Sarah nodded too.

Sergeant Richards asked June, 'You see this boy pelt Overseer Beardsley's daughter, this child?' He was pointing to Sarah.

June searched her father's face and when he nodded, she nodded and answered, 'Yes, but...'

Boysie said, 'Muluk, jus' answer yes or no, don't say nothing else.'

She answered, 'Yes.'

The sergeant asked Ralph. 'You pelt her?' Ralph sulked and answered, 'Yes.'

'Why you pelt her? She provoke you?'

'Yes.'

'How she provoke you?'

'Well, she di'n provoke me the same day but before, whenever I pass the yard she does pelt me and call me coolie.'

'And you used to pelt her back?'

'No, because security guard does always stand up and watch.'

'And the security guard never stop she?'

'No.'

'And why you pelt her the day before the strike?'

'Because she come out the yard, and she call me coolie and the security guard di' gone.'

The sergeant asked Sarah, 'Is true?'

Sarah replied, 'I don't understand.'

'What you don't understand?' the sergeant demanded.

'The way you speak.'

Overseer Beardsley snapped at his daughter. 'Sarah, don't be so impertinent! Answer the sergeant! You understand well enough! You understand the servants! Did you provoke that boy now or didn't you?'

Sarah's bottom lip quivered and she nodded then burst into tears and ran to the jeep into her father's arms. The sergeant questioned Lavender about whether she knew if Sarah did this thing regularly and Lavender replied that it was true, but she added that children who passed by the overseer's house also abused Sarah when she was only standing at the fence watching them go home from school.

The sergeant was satisfied with the children's answers and he turned to the crowd and declared that he was letting Ralph go on the basis of what the children had said, and not on no overseer's, governor's, or anybody else's orders, and he was not doing it because of the ruction they had made here today either; he was the law in this place, no one else.

Overseer Beardsley drove away with his daughter; Ralph went to his mother and they made their way from the compound. Cyrus took June by the hand and led her away too, and Lavender disappeared behind the station to help her father.

16 DIWALI

June did not see Ralph again until Diwali. She had gone back to school by then and was grappling with the learning of British history, geography, and English language and literature, although the British were beginning to leave the country and talk about the coming of the Russians continued. She was becoming accustomed to the ritual of bicycling away from Canefields every morning, accustomed to journeying to New Amsterdam and returning to New Dam every afternoon.

When she cycled to and from the villages she was part of the movement between country and town. It was a continual movement of people which did not allow her to feel alone, a movement which the journey was witness to day after day. If in the end she did not have to remember the lessons which she learnt in the classroom, she would be sure to remember this movement of people of which she had been a part. The habit of memory on her daily journeys became her own discipline, separate from her parents, from the school and the politics of the country.

It was the darkest night of November which was always chosen for Diwali, so that the symbolism of the lights was felt more intensely, and the meaning of exile and return deepened. In the afternoon she was allowed to visit Nani where the children gathered to prepare *deyas* with mud gathered from the backdam, coconut oil and strings of cotton. As they made the *deyas* and sat them out to dry in the sun, Nani retold the story of Rama's exile in the forest. As she recited the story, it seemed to lift her to another plane and she rolled the legend off her tongue like a visionary, conjuring the mythical scenes so that the children felt they were hearing them for the first time: the myth of the Indian kings, queens, princesses, princes, and the Indian empires of Koshala and Sri Lanka; the movement of royal deities between the celestial and the earthly, between exile and return, their confrontations with humanity and nature; saddhus, an army of monkeys, messenger birds, the monumental battle between Hanuman the monkey god and Ravana the demon king of Sri Lanka. The myth absorbed the humiliations of their plantation existence and for one day they swept and cleaned their houses as if they were cleaning away their own exile and its injuries, bearing the lights to light their own way on their own patch of earth, hoping that Lakshmi, the goddess of prosperity and good luck would visit them that night and bless every lighted house. They would wear their best clothes, buy new pots, pay off all their debts, and exchange sweetmeats in the streets.

On this Diwali, Cyrus and Lucille borrowed Mitch's car and took June to see the Corentyne for the first time. The Corentyne strip of road was better than Canefields'. The houses in the crowded villages were bigger, and along the empty stretches of road, where cattle grazed on the flat land, there were the large houses of the few powerful local families, set so far back on the horizon they looked like miniatures suspended between the sky and the land.

Rose Hall was the main town on the Corentyne, not a colonial town like New Amsterdam, but a sugar estate town, the only one of its kind, Cyrus explained. There were few handmade *deyas* and they were overshadowed by the strings of electric bulbs which framed the facades of the shops and houses. They arrived in the town just as the lights came on, and with them, the jukeboxes, and the squibs and small fireworks let off by the gangs of young men gathered outside the shops.

When they returned to New Dam, the lights lit their way back to Mitch's. The *deyas* glowed the more brightly in the great darkness; the hurricane lamps did not need to be lit that night. The lights were especially thick on the ground, along the paths, the bridges, the public road, culverts, and in the parapets – every dark spot was searched out and a light placed there; it created a glow on the earth itself which seemed to suspend the people as they went to and fro with bowls of sweetmeat; it seemed to suspend the houses too. The myth of exile was alive.

She joined the children on the paths, running from cottage to cottage to replace the oil and wicks, racing each other to keep the lights alive and prolong the night. When their parents began to call them indoors and the last *deya* was refilled, June found herself on Nani's landing which looked out across the whole village. She took in the lights on the roof-tops, landings, windows, stairs and in every yard, on the ground everywhere. On this one night of the year, the darkness was completely banished from New Dam and the power of the lights gave a feeling of hope and happiness which she felt the more for the feelings of loss and the dramas of the year.

GLOSSARY

Achchi bat kaho! — Speak good words!
Apko dekani aya — I came to see you
Apna kam khua karo — Do your work yourself
Apra path padho — Read your lessons
Aray bapray — O My God!
Aum bam asi astu — Let my tongue speak, ears hear, nose inhale, eyes see. (The beginning of a prayer).
bachcha — child
badi bahin — big sister
badom ka adar karo — Give respect to the elders.
bahin — sister
bap — father
bedi — a domestic shrine
beti — daughter
chitti — letter
Chup raho! — Keep quiet!
Ghar jao. Sada sukhu raho — Go home. Always be happy.
havan — a sacrifice of material offerings
Jago! — Wake up!
Jamin se utho — Get up from the floor.
Jor se mat bolo — Don't speak loudly.
kata — cloth-pad worn by cane-cutter under their hats to cushion the weight of the cane bundles.
kalam — pen
kamij — shirt
Kan khao! — Eat less!
kapda — skirt
Kisi ki ninda rnat karo! — Don't abuse anybody.
madarsa — school
Maim Hindi sikha hun — I learnt to speak Hindi.
Meri bat suno! — Hear my words!

nani — grandmother
paisa — Indian coin
pirahi — low, backless stool
Sab ko pyar karo — Love all.
santosh — well, happy
Saph kapde pahan — Wear clean clothes.
Tum kal karoje? — What will you do tomorrow?
vidvan — scholar

Other books by Peepal Tree you might enjoy:

Meiling Jin
Song of the Boatwoman
November 1996, Price: STG£6.95 / US$12 / CAN$17
0-948833-86-6, 144 pages

'... She felt like a bird in a cage with the door open. Was she going to fly out?'

Alice, like the other women in Meiling Jin's stories, is at a point of change: Li li is pregnant, alone and frightened at the 'School for Perfect Secretaries'; Gladys plots revenge against her racist neighbour; Margret, taking a trip back home to Malaysia, doesn't know if she can tell her mother that she is a lesbian; Hazel is not sure if her future lies with Sandra and 'a loving which scared her'. Whether her scene is London, China, California, Malaysia or the Caribbean, whether writing with unwavering and painful realism, wicked humour or lyrical imagination, Meiling Jin takes us inside the lives and experiences of her characters in ways which cannot but involve the reader.

Each has a journey to make, each their song to sing. Female or male, lesbian or straight, black or white, all are in some part boatwomen.

Meiling Jin was born in Guyana in 1963, she now lives in London. She is the author of *Gifts from My Grandmother*, a collection of poetry published by Sheba, and stories for children. She is also a playwright and film maker.

Denise Harris
Web of Secrets
May 1996, Price: STG£6.95 / US$12 / CAN$17
0-948833-87-4, 175 pages

'I am Margaret Saunders... call me the eavesdropper...' No-
one tells Margaret anything openly — what has happened to
her father, the cancer taking over her mother's body and why
her grandmother starts seeing faces pressing through invisible
cracks in her bedroom wall. So, with an intuitive sense that
uncovering the truth will free the household from its bondage,
Margaret starts hiding in cupboards and under beds. But as an
'over-imaginative' 14 year old who is, in her family's view,
refusing to grow up, she is acutely vulnerable to feeling that
she is in some way responsible for what she uncovers...

Set in Guyana in midst of the 1960s racial disturbances, *Web
of Secrets* makes suggestive connections between divisions in
the family and the nation. It embroiders a dazzling fabric of
whispered family conversations, fantasy and Guyanese folk-
lore. It warns of the psychic hazards of trying to suppress the
past and proclaims the redemptive power of truth in the
process of healing.

Lakshmi Persaud
Butterfly in the Wind ★Reprinted 3 times★
1990, Price: STG£6.99 / US$12 / CAN$17
0-948833-36-X, 208 pages

From early in her life Kamla is surprised by a contrary inner
voice which frequently gainsays the wisdom of her elders and
betters. But Kamla is growing up in a traditional Hindu
community and attending schools in colonial Trinidad where
rote learning is still the order of the day. She learns that this
voice creates nothing but trouble and silences it. In this book
the voice is freed.

Set in the 1940s, *Butterfly in the Wind* was enthusiastically
received when it first appeared in 1990. Its portrayal of a
passage from childhood to young womanhood was praised by
The Sunday Times as 'a sweet-natured book which is above all
a tremendous celebration of life'. *The Observer* praised it for
'the empathy with which Lakshmi Persaud writes of the
natural world ... and Hindu customs'. *India Weekly* wrote that
Lakshmi Persaud 'maintains the high tradition of Indian
Caribbean writing set by V. S. Naipaul', and *Time Out* found
it 'packed with memories of everyday life from family rela-
tionships to schoolday traumas'.

Narmala Shewcharan
Tomorrow is Another Day
March 1994, Price: STG£6.95 / US$12 / CAN$17
0-948833-47-5, 238 pages

They were all beggars at the gate, thinks Asha, as she joins the vast queue for visas outside the American Embassy. In a corrupt, seedy dictatorship, whose citizens feel It's a prison outside too, what else is there to do? But the option of escape is not open to, or desired by all. There are other choices to be made. Should Jagru quit the opposition and try to influence the ruling party from within? When will Manu's luck with smuggling run out? Where is Lal's duty? With his family or fighting the Government? Is Chandi's concern with her children enough? Without imposing easy judgements, Narmala Shewcharan takes us inside the choices her characters make, and their price. This skilfully constructed novel movingly portrays the human costs of social fragmentation, but also asserts the moral basis of community in the impact each individual choice has on the lives of others.

Narmala Shewcharan was born in Guyana where she worked as a journalist. She now lives in Britain.

Peepal Tree Press publishes a wide selection of outstanding fiction, poetry, drama, history and literary criticism with a focus on the Caribbean, Africa, the South Asian diaspora and Black life in Britain. Peepal Tree is now the largest independent publisher of Caribbean writing in the world. All our books are high quality original paperbacks designed to stand the test of time and repeated readings.

All Peepal Tree books should be available through your local bookseller, though you are most welcome to place orders direct with us. When ordering a book direct from us, simply tell us the title, author, quantity and the address to which the book should be mailed. Please enclose a cheque or money order for the cover price of the book, plus £1 / US$3.20 / CAN$5.50 towards postage and packing.

Peepal Tree sends out regular e-mail information about new books and special offers. We also produce a yearly catalogue which gives current prices in sterling, US and Canadian dollars and full details of all our books. Contact us to join our mailing list.

You can contact Peepal Tree at:

17 King's Avenue
Leeds LS6 1QS
United Kingdom

e-mail hannah@peepal.demon.co.uk
tel: 44 (0)113 245 1703
fax: 44 (0)113 245 9616

STOP PRESS: **peepaltreepress.com**

From May 2002, come to the Peepal Tree website to buy books on line and use the browse, author information, topic-finder and theme map databases for background information on Peepal Tree titles